ATOLL X

RUSSELL JAMES

SEVEREDPRESS

ATOLL X

Copyright © 2022 by Russell James

WWW.SEVEREDPRESS.COM

ISBN: 978-1-922861-46-7

Dedication

For Christy,
Thanks for all your support in this writing endeavor.

Other books by Russell James

Grant Coleman Adventures
Cavern of the Damned
Monsters in the Clouds
Curse of the Viper King
Forest of Fire
Mammoth Island

Ranger Kathy West National Park Adventures
Claws
Dragons of Kilauea
Ravens of Yellowstone

Rick and Rose Sinclair Adventures
Temple of the Queen of Sheba
Voyage to Blackbeard's Island

CHAPTER ONE

Zachary eased the anchor into the water from the sailboat's bow. It slipped into the Pacific without a sound. Link by link, he played out first the chain and then the nylon line attached to it. At twenty feet, the anchor hit the reef. Zachary gave the line a tug and set the flukes fast. He let another forty feet of line slither out through his hands and then wrapped the rope around the bow cleat. He stood up and grabbed the sloop's forward stay for support.

A seemingly infinite number of stars sparkled in the night sky, even with the full moon low on the horizon. The calm sea sent gentle waves lapping at the shore of the atoll fifty yards off the bow.

His girlfriend Gracie came forward from the cockpit. She was eighteen, just a few months younger than he was. Her hair was back in a ponytail and she wore a faded T-shirt and cargo shorts. He still thought she looked cute as hell.

"I can't believe we sailed across open ocean for days and actually found this place," she said.

"Give the credit to GPS and my years of sailing lessons off Martha's Vineyard."

His conservative father had paid for those sailing lessons, and would be furious if he knew that Zachary had used those skills in the service of Green Warriors. The eco-terrorist group had sourced this thirty-foot sloop out of Tonga so Zachary and Gracie could execute a two-person recon of what everyone called Atoll X.

"Everyone else's Senior Summer will be totally lame compared to ours," she said.

"We'll be radically famous after this," Zachary said.

He imagined the glowing international press they'd garner. Atoll X was privately owned by billionaire Parker Rothman. He'd declared it a nature and marine sanctuary, off-limits to all. Green Warriors didn't trust that he was actually doing that. They had sent Zachary and Gracie to blow the lid off whatever this entitled elitist was up to.

Zachary led Gracie back to the inflatable raft tied off at the stern. Their backpacks were already stowed in the bow. There was no point in locking the cabin up when they left. It wasn't like anyone was going to sail by and steal anything. The two climbed into the raft, Gracie in the front and Zachary in the rear. Gracie cast them off, and they began paddling to shore.

As they got closer, the rising moon better lit their destination. A white sand beach seemed to glow in the moonlight. Beyond it, curved palm trees looked like they were too tired to hold their fronds straight up. Scrubby vegetation covered the ground between the trees. An off-shore breeze kissed Zachary's face with the scent of orchids.

While Zachary had years of experience on the water, Gracie had none. So, where Zachary dipped his paddle into the sea and made strong, silent strokes, Gracie produced more sound than propulsion as her paddle slapped at the water. Zachary hadn't expected much more and didn't bother to coach her. He'd invited her for her performance in bed, not for her maritime skills. They'd be ashore soon anyway, and stealth didn't matter getting to an empty beach.

The raft's nose hit the sand and Gracie got out. She cried out in pain.

"What's wrong?" Zachary said.

"My foot! I cut my foot."

Zachary turned on his flashlight. Gracie's shoes sat in the bow of the raft. He couldn't believe her stupidity.

"The coral is sharp as hell," he said. "Why did you take your shoes off?"

"I didn't want them to get wet."

The whine in her voice made Zachary even madder. "Let me see."

She raised her foot out of the water and into the beam of Zachary's flashlight. She'd managed to earn herself a nice gash along her heel. Blood ran down her foot and dripped off her toes into the water.

"Damn it. Get up on the beach."

Gracie hopped out of the water and up onto the sand. Zachary threw her shoes after her, which was as useful as closing the door after the dog got out. He slipped overboard into the warm water and pulled the raft half out of the water. With a disgusted sigh, he tossed her backpack at her feet.

"Put a bandage on that so we can get going."

He paced the beach as she patted dry her foot and then fumbled with her flashlight and the bandage at the same time. Tiny waves lapped the shore like the ticking of a clock. He was really beginning to regret not bringing someone more useful than Gracie.

The sound of rubber scraping sand made his heart skip a beat. He whirled around to see the raft sliding out into the sea, dragging the rope off the bow like a retreating tail through the sand.

He dropped his flashlight and sprinted for the boat. Just as the bow cleared the beach, he dove on the line and grabbed it with both hands. He exhaled in relief. A rogue wave must have lifted it off the beach. With his backpack still in the bow, having the raft sail off on its own was the last thing he needed.

The rope in his hand went taut. He pulled. The rope stretched. The raft didn't move.

"What the hell?"

He'd just paddled the thing in here without going aground. There was no way it was hung up on anything, especially since it rode higher in the water with no one in it.

His flashlight was several feet away in the sand, so he could only see the general outline of the raft. Its silhouette included some kind of bulge at the stern. He wrapped the rope around his wrist for a better bite and pulled hard on it again. The raft still didn't budge.

He turned to call for Gracie to help. She was still sitting in the sand, whimpering as she taped a bandage in place over her sliced foot.

"Gracie! Help me with the raft!"

"I can't get this bandage to stick. My skin is too wet or something."

3

Zachary gritted his teeth. She wasn't going to be any help now, and quite possibly for the entire trip. He dug in his heels in preparation to give the rope a solid pull.

Then the rope pulled at him. The force knocked him off balance.

"No way," he said to himself. "The current isn't strong enough to—"

The raft jerked out to sea. The line he'd wrapped around his wrist tightened and yanked him off his feet. He slammed face-down in the sand.

The raft rushed out to sea. Zachary skidded down the beach face-first, and then plowed into the water. Sand sluiced into his shirt and pants. Saltwater rushed into his mouth and set his throat on fire. He choked, rolled onto his back, and stretched upward in search of air.

He surfaced with the back of his head cutting through the water like the prow of a boat. He sucked in a gulp of salty air. His back grazed a reef and coral slashed at his spine. A boom cracked through the night as one of the raft compartments exploded. The rope went slack, and Zachary began to sink.

His feet did not touch bottom. He swam up and broke the surface. He was dozens of yards from the shore. From the beach came the sound of Gracie screaming his name at a pitch he didn't think human beings could reach.

His back burned. His shoulders ached from likely dislocation. Saltwater and sand sloshed in his stomach. He treaded water and unwound the rope from his wrist. Warm blood wept from the rope burn.

How could so much go so wrong so quickly? he thought.

He began a pained swim for shore. Every rotation of his shoulders felt like grit grinding in gears. He rolled over on his back and switched to a slow, sculling backstroke instead.

"Zachary!" Gracie cried out.

He moaned out a reply he doubted she could hear.

Her flashlight beam played back and forth across the water in a series of jerky, panicked sweeps. The beam passed him several times and then spotlighted his head.

"Zachary!"

4

Zachary wanted to respond but it was all he could do to just keep breathing and swimming.

Two yards beyond his feet at the edge of the flashlight beam, twin mounds rose from the surface a few feet apart. They followed him.

Zachary's pulse raced. He kicked harder and faster but the two lumps gained on him. Gracie's flashlight beam moved from his head to the water behind him. The mounds glistened scaly and wet.

"Zachary? There's something—"

Lids rolled up on the mounds to reveal two glowing yellow eyes with slit pupils. Gracie shrieked. Zachary froze in shock.

The water behind him exploded like a depth charge had gone off. All the flashlight lit up was white water. Zachary felt an unbelievable force clamp down on his chest. Ribs cracked and all the air was squeezed from his lungs in a rush. The creature pulled him underwater and the last thing Zachary heard was his girlfriend's muffled wail.

CHAPTER TWO

Professor Grant Coleman was thrilled to be back in his office at Robeson University. He taught paleontology and his goal between now and fall semester was to catch up on journals and catalog some new finds with his grad students.

The relaxing Hawaiian vacation he'd planned for the summer had instead turned into a week of dodging wooly mammoths and saber-tooth cats in the Arctic. Death-defying escapes from wild animals were not what he called relaxing. He wanted to stop falling into terrifying adventures like that before they became a habit.

His small office might have looked like a glorious mess to any visitor, but each teetering pile contained strata of the previous semester's events. He didn't always remember exactly what was in each pile, but he had long ago rationalized that the time spent searching for a few things was far less than the time he would have spent properly filing everything. He slid one pile a few inches to the left to make room to prop his feet up on his desk. Today's limited agenda included catching up on a paper a colleague had done on trilobite evolution and a long overdue cheeseburger at his favorite place just off campus. Summer meant not having to wait in line behind a dozen students to order one.

His phone rang. Caller ID announced it was Harvey Rindzunner, his literary agent. Grant's near-death experiences had spawned a series of adventure novels he'd written where a college professor battled giant monsters. The pulpy sci-fi books weren't successful enough to let him quit his teaching job, but they acted as therapy after his ordeals and the royalties did help keep his ex-wife's alimony payments at bay.

Grant wasn't in the mood to talk about writing, but Harvey had some literary irons in the fire for him, and Grant was curious about how hot they were getting. He answered the phone.

"Hey, Harvey."

"Grant, my man. How is the trans-Pacific traveler? Good trip to your island paradise?"

"Colder than I expected, but the wildlife was entertaining."

"Hope you came back with inspiration for your next novel."

"You have no idea," Grant said. "How about the projects you are working on for my current novels?"

"Through the roof, my man. Things are really happening."

That raised Grant's spirits. "You got the movie deal for *Monsters in the Clouds*?"

"No, that fell through."

"The television pilot for *Curse of the Viper King*?"

"The studio decided to focus more on sitcoms."

"The foreign translation rights for *Forest of Fire*?"

"Tough sell. You kind of pissed off the Chinese government with that one."

Really? Grant thought. *The bastards did try to kill me when I was in their country.*

"So how are you defining 'really happening' then?" Grant said.

"Glad you asked. You'll be so pumped over this. Private consultant gig with billionaire Parker Rothman as he digs up some…" Keyboard keys tapped in the background. "…itchy thorax?"

"*Ichthyosaur*," Grant corrected. "A giant reptile fish from the Mesozoic era."

"Sure. Mesotastic, right. Anyhow, he's building an eco-friendly resort in the Pacific called Nirvana Island, wants a consultant to curate a display of the fossils they found during construction. There's talk of a documentary with you as the expert. Really boost your brand recognition."

"I don't know. I don't want to be some ignorant businessman's private scientist."

"Remember what that movie deal would have been worth?" Harvey said.

"I don't forget numbers like that."

"He's paying double that for two week's work, plus expenses."

Grant arched an eyebrow. That was pay-off-the-mortgage money. But in Grant's experience, all his side gigs never seemed to go as planned.

"And," Harvey added, "he owns Sable Palm Studios. They make big budget pictures. Doesn't hurt to have him know who you are."

Perhaps Harvey had lined up a winner for him after all.

"All I'm doing is cataloging fossils and putting them in displays?" Grant said.

"Absolutely. You won't even break a sweat."

"I can break a sweat watching TV."

"Look, Grant," Harvey said in the therapist voice he always adopted for the hard sell, "I can't help you if you don't want to help yourself."

Grant pondered the offer. "Okay, I'll do it."

"Good, because I already signed the contract. Airline tickets are on the way. You leave in August and will be back before school restarts. Talk to you soon."

Harvey disconnected. Grant stared at his phone.

Won't even break a sweat, he thought. Maybe his personal life adventures were making him paranoid, but he already had a feeling that he should have passed on this supposedly simple job.

CHAPTER THREE

By the time August arrived, Grant had psyched himself up for Nirvana Island. This was going to be the kind of working vacation he'd dreamed about. Good pay, short hours, and the grunt work of digging the fossils up had already been done. The letter accompanying his tickets boasted that the resort was mostly complete and there would be first-class dining onsite as the chef worked out all the restaurant recipes. He hoped cheeseburgers were somewhere on the menu. Bacon cheeseburgers would be even better.

Standing in the security line at the airport, he saw his reflection in the glass along the wall. He looked more tourist than professor in jeans, sandals, and a Hawaiian-style shirt. He gave the shirt a tug, but it still struggled to cover his paunchy stomach. His resolution to start hitting the gym hadn't worked itself up to the top of his to-do list for some reason. He'd definitely start when he got back. What better time than with a new semester? And what better time than after spending two weeks being fed by a gourmet chef?

He straightened his glasses and took a closer look at the reflection of his hairline. Had it receded more? He was ready to blame monster-related stress for that. Two weeks at Nirvana Island Resort might just get those follicles motivated to get back to work.

He passed through the security scanners and endured partial disrobing as he daydreamed about what his destination would be like. He finished putting his shoes back on and headed for his gate.

"Grant Coleman?" said a woman behind him.

He turned around to see an attractive woman with long blonde hair who was about his age. He smiled.

He was a relatively accomplished paleontologist, and his monster novels, while not literary genius, had developed a small devoted group of readers. Between those two, he'd hoped that someday in a public space, he'd be recognized by a stranger for his professional accomplishments. Having it be by an attractive woman was certainly a plus. He adopted a look that he was sure seemed suave.

"Yes, I'm Dr. Coleman," he said.

She frowned and shoved his backpack against his chest. The tag on the handle had his name on it in big red letters. "You left this on the chair back there. That's the kind of dumbass move that gets people calling TSA and delaying all our flights."

She walked away shaking her head the way she likely did when one of her kids did something stupid.

"Thank you," he said.

It looked like today wasn't going to be the day he turned famous.

The shifting time zones masked the actual numbers, but flying halfway around the world sure seemed to take a long time. Sure, it beat the hell out of sailing with Ferdinand Magellan in a wooden ship, but it was still interminable. Various connections in the states eventually delivered him to American Samoa, where he hopped a flight for the last five hundred miles or so to Tonga. By the time he landed, he wasn't sure what time it was, what day it was, and even the year seemed a little fuzzy.

He stepped off of the plane and was met by one of the gate agents. She wore a red blazer and had an air of officiality to her.

"Professor Coleman?"

"Every day," Grant said, "though I awaken each morning hoping for something better."

She didn't react to his joke. He sighed at the poor sense of humor most people had.

"If you could follow me," she said, "I'll take you to your connection. Your luggage is already being transferred."

Grant's face brightened. This was a far cry from manhandling his luggage on a mad dash between gates to make a connection. Grant thought he could easily get used to this kind of treatment.

She took him down a set of steps and out a door to the apron around the terminal. Just ahead sat a gleaming white helicopter. The tail boom had ROTHMAN ENTERPRISES painted on it in red letters. The sleek design made the helicopter look fast just sitting still. The rear sliding door stood open and revealed two captain's chairs in the carpeted passenger area.

"This is for me?" Grant said.

"Yes, sir. Mr. Rothman generally spares no expense."

"Mr. Rothman and I need to work together more often."

He climbed aboard and settled into the plush leather chair. The seat was more comfortable than his recliner at home. The gate agent rolled the door closed.

The last time he'd been in a helicopter, he'd sat in a stiff canvas seat with a freezing wind blowing snow in his face. Someone had just tried to kill him and he'd barely escaped an attack by saber-tooth tigers before that. He could already tell this trip was going to be very different.

The pilot handed him a headset from the front seat. Grant put it on.

"I'm Carla," she said. "Welcome aboard. We'll be at the resort about an hour and a half after takeoff."

"Where is this place?"

"Nirvana Island is just under two hundred and fifty miles southeast of Tonga."

"The name certainly promises a lot."

"Mr. Rothman renamed it when he bought it," Carla said, "but I promise you that it will live up to the title. Strap yourself in and stay seated for the flight. Sit back and relax."

"If you insist," Grant said.

Carla was true to her word. For over an hour, they flew over empty ocean. Grant didn't see a boat of any kind on the water or even another aircraft in the sky. Then he caught sight of islands up ahead.

As they got closer, he corrected himself. The larger mass wasn't an island. It was a huge atoll. Atolls occurred when coral began to grow in a ring around an island. Over time, coral grew and the island subsided and sank. After tens of thousands of years or more, what was left looked from the air like a donut, a giant ring of coral with a lagoon in the center. Sand and vegetation sometimes set up shop to create tiny islands.

Weather and waves usually pounded most atolls into a set of broken crescents, on rare occasions perhaps a near-closed circle with a bit of shelter in the center for a visiting ship. But this atoll was the one-in-a million example. It was a wide, complete ring around a deep lagoon miles across. The widest parts of the atoll were at least a mile across and filled with tropical jungle. The narrowest section was bone-white and less than a hundred yards wide. Grant couldn't believe he'd never heard of this atoll given its unique features.

"That's a perfect atoll to build a resort," Grant said. "What's its name?"

"It doesn't have a name. We jokingly refer to it as Atoll X. Mr. Rothman set it aside as a wildlife preserve. The resort is on the smaller island to the right."

Grant looked out the other window. A few miles away from the atoll, a hilly, banana-shaped island poked out of the blue Pacific. The island's inner crescent had a white beach so dazzling it looked like it was made of diamonds. Lush forest carpeted the island's interior, though a few dirt roads had been cut across it.

The helicopter descended and turned for the island. As they got closer, the amazing details of the resort became discernable. A dock stretched out from the beach into the sea. Where the dock met the beach, a boardwalk ran up to the resort building. The enormous structure mirrored the curve of the beach in front of it. Some kind of faux-thatch edged the roof, surrounding solar panels and probably obscuring them from a ground-level view. The exterior appeared to be sheathed in polished teak. The stair-step design had three floors. The second and third floors looked like the guest rooms, with each one having a private balcony overlooking the ocean. To the rear, a huge, kidney-shaped pool acted as the centerpiece for exquisite landscaping.

The pilot lined the aircraft up to the left of the building, aiming for a concrete pad with a big H painted on it. The helicopter landed light as a feather settling to the ground. Rotor wash sent up a halo of white sand around the helipad.

"Out you go," Carla said. "Your bag is at the rear of the compartment."

Grant saw his suitcase behind the chairs. He pulled on the handle and slid the rear door open. It was odd that no one was here to greet him. The helicopter pilot would have radioed in their arrival. Maybe no one wanted to brave the rotor-induced sandstorm.

"Walk straight ahead until you are outside the rotor disk," Carla said, "so I know where you are before I take off. Enjoy your stay."

Grant headed for the door. He forgot to take his headset off. The cord went tight and jerked his head straight back. He took off the headset and passed it to the pilot. She shook her head at his clumsiness.

Sometimes his gift for being uncool amazed even himself.

He hauled his roller board out of the helicopter and slid the door shut. Grant lugged the suitcase past the nose of the helicopter and into the sand outside the helipad. He turned around to give the pilot a wave.

She didn't care. Before he could make eye contact, the helicopter lifted straight up. Rotor wash sandblasted his face and coated his glasses in dirt. Above him, the helicopter nosed over and screamed away in the direction of Tonga.

The dust settled and the noise of the helicopter dialed down to nothing. Grant cleaned his glasses with his shirt, aware that it was just as gritty, but he had no other options. He spit the dirt from his lips and put his glasses back on.

No concierge stood ready to greet him. No bellboy dashed over to take his bag. In fact, he didn't see a soul anywhere.

As far as Grant could tell, he was alone on this island.

CHAPTER FOUR

Grant dragged his roller board through the sand until he got to the paved sidewalk. He pulled it up on the concrete and continued. One wheel squeaked and then stopped turning as sand froze up the bearings. He continued pulling the bag forward with twice the effort as the rough surface sanded the bottom of that wheel flat.

At the main entrance, two glass doors whooshed open and a blast of frosty air washed over him. He stepped inside to a marble floor polished to a mirror-like finish. A long teak counter straight ahead had a variety of tropical animals and plants carved into the front. Wicker furniture to the right and left created welcoming conversation space among potted palms. Behind the counter hung a painting of the resort under blues skies and a bright sun.

This all looked wonderful, except for the lack of staff and a wall clock that had stopped running at 2:45.

A small desktop bell sat on the counter. He'd never seen someone ring one of those and not look like an entitled jackass doing it.

"Hello?" he called out instead.

A slight Asian man in khaki shorts and a bright blue Nirvana Island Resort golf shirt scurried around to the counter. His dark hair was cut very short on the sides but swelled to a brush cut on the top of his head. He looked surprised to see Grant. More so when he saw he had a suitcase.

"I thought I heard the helicopter," he said, "but I wasn't expecting anyone, especially a guest. We're not open yet."

"I'm supposed to be helping make that opening happen," Grant said. "I'm Professor Grant Coleman, here to curate some fossil exhibits."

"Oh, my. That was moved to next month at the earliest. You weren't contacted? Hold on." The man pulled a thick ledger book out from under the counter, flipped open some pages and ran his finger down a list of handwritten entries. "Yes, I left a message for Mr. Harvey Rindzunner last week with the new dates and instructions on how to change the tickets."

"That's my agent. It's nice to know my voicemails aren't the only ones that he ignores. The helicopter pilot didn't get the word either."

"She was watching for your ticketed arrival. When you didn't change the flight, she was still there to pick you up." He extended a hand. "I am Hisoka Nishimura, the manager, though lately I feel like a construction project engineer."

Grant gave the well-appointed lobby a once over. "Looks like you're doing a fine job."

"We finished this area first for all the publicity photos. Follow me."

He led Grant to the hallway behind the lobby. Absent ceiling tiles exposed ductwork and wiring behind a grid of silver metal frames. Unfinished sheetrock covered the walls. The lovely marble tile stopped halfway down the hallway, revealing unfinished concrete.

"Everything is behind schedule," Hisoka said. "This will be the display area for the fossils, so our guests can see them as they head to their rooms. You'll have to imagine them both sitting in display cases and hanging on the walls here."

Imagining that was a tall order, but Grant gave it a try. There would have to be some big fossils to make it work.

"The fossils are at the end of this hall in Conference Room B," Hisoka said. "All the tools you requested are there as well. I'll unlock the door for you in the morning."

From the other end of the hall came a tall black man in tan cargo shorts and a matching safari-type shirt. If Grant had made true on all his promises to hit the gym over the years, he would have had this man's physique by now, with bulging biceps and a narrow waist. A pistol hung from a holster on one hip. His head was shaved and fire burned in his dark eyes.

"Who is this?" he said to Hisoka.

"Professor Coleman. Here to curate the fossil collection."

The man looked Grant over. "You're not supposed to be here for weeks. We're not prepared for you."

"No problem," Grant said. "I'm used to being unwelcome wherever I go. My agent never told me about the schedule change."

"Grant," Hisoka said, "this is Allen Eastman, head of security."

Grant shook his hand. He was sure he heard his bones crush in the man's grip.

"The island needs armed security?" Grant said. "It's kind of in the middle of nowhere."

"Which is why it needs armed security," Allen said. "We're a private island, with no protection from any government here in international waters. We could have problems ranging from casual trespassers to pirates."

"Pirates? I thought they hijacked tankers and big ships like that."

"In some places they do. Here they prefer to kidnap for ransom. We don't want to be a target for that, or to have them use our islands as a place to avoid authorities while they wait for their money."

Grant had been so taken by the idea of a little island paradise that he hadn't thought about how vulnerable an isolated place like this could be.

"Then I'm glad you're here to stop that," he said.

Hisoka checked his watch. "It's time for dinner. Let's grab something to eat and then I'll set you up in your room."

"I'm not known for turning down food," Grant said.

A lot of this little trip might have been unravelling, but the promise of first-class fare for dinner was going to salve a lot of wounds. Grant had been living on cold airplane food and peanuts for what seemed like days.

Hisoka led the three of them down the hall. They stopped in front of two large wooden doors. In thick, black magic marker on the sheetrock someone had handwritten DINING ROOM. Grant had a bad feeling about what was on the other side of the door.

Hisoka opened the door and put Grant's fears to rest. The dining room looked magnificent. A central skylight lit the room and live tropical plants hung from the ceiling. Circular tables in rich, dark wood surrounded a long table and chairs in the center of the room. Three people were already seated at the main table.

"Everyone," Hisoka announced, "this is Professor Grant Coleman. He'll be curating the fossil display."

Grant saw disappointment settle on every face at the table. He realized how out of place his garish vacation outfit was. Everyone wore casual, durable clothes, like they had serious work to do. From the condition of their clothing, it looked like they had been doing that work.

"I assumed by the look of you that you weren't the electrical engineer I'm waiting on," a stout man said.

He rose and came to Grant. They shook hands. Fair-skinned and freckled, a Tampa Bay Rays baseball cap did a poor job covering his shock of red hair.

"I'm John McGinty," he said. "Managing the construction."

"And managing to fall behind," a man in what looked like a cruise ship officer's uniform said.

McGinty shot him a silencing glance. "Mr. Rothman makes changes that are way outside the project scope, and then that screws up the schedule. And I can't exactly zip over to Home Depot and pick a few things up. Everything has to get shipped through three ports before it gets to Tonga and then to us. Plus, some of these last-minute bright ideas require redesign. Which is why I was hoping you were the electrical engineer."

"Sorry to disappoint on that one," Grant said.

"This is Captain Wilson," Hisoka said, gesturing to the man in pseudo-uniform.

Wilson seemed to be in his thirties, with none of the weather-beaten seafaring-look Grant would expect in a sea captain. His blond hair looked like it had been styled for the cover of GQ magazine and he had a long, narrow nose that gave him a patrician air. He seemed too thin to be hauling in anchor lines and battening down hatches in a storm.

"I captain the *Endeavor*," Wilson said. "It is Mr. Rothman's boat he keeps here at the island. We make runs to Tonga for resupply, that kind of thing."

"Cargo vessel?" Grant said.

"Luxury yacht," McGinty said. "A rich man's overcompensation for something."

"And yet it keeps supplies coming in like clockwork," Wilson said.

The third man stepped up to Grant's other side. "I'm Kaelo Palu."

Where McGinty was stout, Kaelo was a brick wall, a Polynesian sumo wrestler wrapped in muscle. He had his long black hair pulled back in a ponytail that accentuated his high broad cheekbones. Decorative tattoos covered his forearms.

"I'm here for two reasons," Kaelo said. "First, to make sure that these mainlanders don't put something embarrassing into the design."

"Such as?"

"There was a plan to put what they thought was an inspirational quote in Tongan on one wall. It was actually a pretty filthy insult about someone's mother."

Grant couldn't help but smile. "The second reason?"

"To make sure any discoveries of previous Tongan settlements here are preserved."

"This is pretty far for Tongans to have paddled to."

"The Tongans crisscrossed the Pacific," Kaelo said, "visiting many islands. There's no record we were here, but there's a good chance we were."

"The Tongan traditions are something passed down through your family?"

"That and I have a doctorate of Anthropology from the University of Melbourne."

Grant felt his face redden at assuming the man opposite him had no higher education.

Kaelo smiled and jabbed him in the shoulder. "It's cool, bro. You Westerners think we're all witch doctors and volcano worshippers."

"This isn't everyone on the island, is it?" Grant asked Hisoka, eager to get the conversation transitioned to something, anything, less embarrassing.

"No, there are twenty or so people working construction, some cooks, and the *Endeavor's* crew. We leaders meet here for meals each day."

Twin doors to the kitchen swung open and a petite woman in an unbuttoned, white chef's coat stepped into the room. Her black hair was up in a bun at the back of her head and a hairnet covered it. She had piercing blue eyes and a mole on one cheek that Grant thought looked adorable.

"Marie LaRue," Hisoka said. "Our head chef who comes straight from the finest restaurants in Paris. Marie, this is Professor Coleman, our paleontologist."

"Nice to meet you," she said.

"I've been looking forward to your cooking," Grant said.

"You won't be getting any of it tonight," she said.

Behind her, a cook in whites pushed a cart through the doors and wheeled it over to the table. A brown cardboard box sat on the cart, opened. Inside were footlong brown plastic pouches.

"Hurrah," McGinty deadpanned. "Another round of fine French cuisine. What was this called? Oh yes, *le MRE*."

MRE stood for the military rations called Meals Ready to Eat. Grant had been down that road before. With few exceptions, the entrees were awful, and that assessment was from a man who considered Pop Tarts good cuisine.

"Well, the solar power was down," Marie said. "Again! I can't cook without electricity, which would be your department, Mr. McGinty."

"The inverters were damaged by saltwater while they were on someone's boat." McGinty looked at Captain Wilson, who looked away. "When one inverter goes down, there's only enough power to keep the essentials going. It's being repaired in the shop and should be online tomorrow."

"A short-term problem," Hisoka said, apparently trying to smooth things over. "A little emergency food will just make Marie's next meal all the more delicious by comparison."

Grant reached in and pulled out a pouch. The label read CHILI WITH BEANS. That was his least favorite among the unfavorites, and the least liked by his digestive tract. He wasn't about to toss it back and pick another given the general unhappiness with the MRE situation and his newcomer status. He kept it and took a seat at the table.

The glass at his setting was crystal, the silverware gleaming and new. The gold rim around the china plate before him was so polished the light reflected off it made him wince. He poured the contents of his pouch onto the plate, a bunch of plastic packets in lovely drab brown.

This is going to be a miserable trip, he thought.

After dinner, Hisoka walked Grant and his suitcase up the stairway to the second floor. Elevators were apparently non-essential systems. They walked down another unfinished corridor to his room. Hisoka opened the door without having to use a keycard.

"The doors aren't locked?" Grant said.

"No power to the lock system or the wi-fi to run it yet. We are using the honor system and personal trust."

The door opened to a room that was more prison cell than luxury suite. The walls were bare concrete block, the floor rough and unfinished. Two sheets covered a king-sized bed missing a headboard. A single pillow lay at the head of the bed. A small desk with a chair hugged the opposite wall. The air was stale and dusty. The big difference between the room and a dungeon was the sliding glass door at the other side of the room that opened to a balcony.

"There's still a lot of work to do on this room," Hisoka said.

"Horror movie torture rooms look more inviting," Grant said.

"I gave you this one because, despite all the finishing touches it's missing, the bathroom facilities are complete."

"There's something to be said for being able to shower, shave and…take a load off."

Grant walked back to the sliding glass door. He opened it and stepped out to his balcony. It had a view of the landscaped pool area behind the building. His incoming aerial view had been deceiving. The pool bottom had been painted blue and the pool was empty. So much for sitting poolside after work each day.

He stepped back in and started to close the door. Hisoka stopped him.

"You'll want to leave that open. Second floor air conditioning hasn't been installed yet."

Grant looked where a thermostat would be on the wall. Three wires stuck out of the concrete block.

"With the door open, this will be only slightly better than sleeping outside," Grant said. "This is like camping with a toilet."

"After sunset," Hisoka said, "the breeze is surprisingly cool."

"I can't wait," Grant said.

CHAPTER FIVE

The next morning, Grant awoke to brilliant, blinding sunshine. That was when he realized that one of the other amenities his room was missing were drapes. He'd wrapped himself in the sheet at some point in the night. Hisoka had been right, the breeze off the water got downright chilly. He was going to ask for a second sheet today.

A welcome hot shower warmed him right up and he went down to the dining room for breakfast around 8:30. He'd forgotten to ask when breakfast was served. An MRE with his name post-it noted to it sat on the big table next to a bottle of water. He wasn't sure if his was the only pouch left, or if everyone else had arisen earlier, gotten an actual breakfast, and left him this as punishment for sleeping in by their standards.

He checked the bag's label. Spaghetti and Meatballs. Everyone's favorite breakfast food. He didn't see any point in sitting alone in the dining room scooping his meal out of a pouch, so he took his poor excuse for a breakfast out in the hall. He turned left and headed down to the conference room that Hisoka had said housed his fossils. He stopped at a set of double doors with a big letter B written on the wall beside them. The doors had conventional, keyed locks. Grant turned the door handle.

True to his word, Hisoka had left the door unlocked. Grant entered and fumbled along the wall until he found a light switch and flicked it on. His jaw dropped at the sight.

He'd been worried that tiny fossils would be lost in the spacious hallway meant for their display. That fear evaporated. These fossils were huge. The largest was a slab almost nine feet long and five feet wide. Grant went straight to it.

The formation was light sandstone. The attention grabber was the skull at one end of the slab. The long, narrow head carried jaws full of sharp, slashing teeth. Large empty sockets once housed eyes that could see well in low, underwater light. A long, slender neck of uncountable vertebrae made an S shape and disappeared into stone that still encased the body. At the opposite end, a shorter tail appeared and ran almost to the edge of the slab. Grant guessed that if the neck was straightened out, the creature would have been almost twenty feet long.

He'd need to double check a dozen things, but he was pretty sure this would be a *Liopleurodon*, one of the largest, deadliest plesiosaurs to ever swim the seas. Plesiosaurs had long necks and tails, large rounded bodies, and four huge flippers. If he could clear away the stone that encased the animal's body, he could be certain. Given the size of the creature, that simple idea could take a team of paleontologists a year to do properly.

He looked closer at the tail and gasped. An imprint of the animal's skin was still in the stone. It showed the outline of scales, a discovery all by itself that could get Grant international recognition. But it also showed the outline of a spaded tail, likely filled with long-decayed cartilage as a structural frame. That meant this bad boy had used his tail as a highly efficient rudder. Between being able to turn on a dime and simultaneously twist his head in any direction, Grant wondered if any prey could have escaped this predator.

Grant could have spent the whole day examining the plesiosaur. He had to pull himself away from the fossil to inventory the others. Smaller fossils lay on the floor, some in piles. Most were fish he would have to work hard to identify. Some were fossil fragments, just a few bones from a carcass scavenged millions of years ago. To a casual observer, these specimens would inspire no awe. But in each one, Grant saw the potential for a new window into the past, perhaps one more clue to finish the puzzle of how these animals lived.

Another large slab leaned against the far wall. He knelt down in front of it and adjusted his glasses for a better view. This fossil was just a four-foot-long skull, but a remarkably well preserved one. Compared to the plesiosaur, this skull was much more birdlike, with a very long and slender set of jaws. Nasal openings were set between the end of the upper jaw and the massive eye socket that covered most of the skull. Unlike the plesiosaur's broad, blade-like teeth, this creature's teeth were thin, like sharpened pegs.

This was an ichthyosaur, though it would take a lot of work to determine the specific species. Most species had dolphin-like bodies, with large humps behind the heads. Like the plesiosaur, these reptiles were hunters. But by the different tooth evolutions, they sought different prey, ichthyosaurs smaller, softer species, plesiosaurs bigger fish. In fact, there were fossils of plesiosaurs whose stomachs contained ichthyosaur bones.

Every moment of second guessing he'd done about accepting this job had been wasted time. This room was a gold mine. Last night he was worried that he couldn't fill the two weeks he was to spend here. Now he wasn't sure he'd be done by then.

Hisoka had said that all the tools he'd requested would be here. He looked around and saw a stack of boxes in the corner by a work table with a stool. Brushes. Picks. A small vacuum. A set of precision drills. All brand new.

He sat on the stool and took everything in with a satisfied smile.

Hisoka rolled a cart carrying a large box into the room. He looked at Grant with alarm.

"Professor Coleman, is everything all right?"

"Yes, it's perfect. That's an all-too infrequent moment, so I'm savoring it." He looked at Hisoka's cart. "What's in the box?"

"Another fossil, I think. Several workers found it on the beach. One of them was superstitious and took a hammer to it, saying it was a monster and it would draw other monsters to it."

"That wouldn't be the first time people have reacted that way."

"It is damaged beyond repair but I thought you should see it before we tossed it away, just in case."

Hisoka left the room and Grant went over to investigate the fossil in the box. The first thing he noticed was that this artifact wasn't a fossil. Most people see an articulated skeleton in a museum and think that those are bones, when actually they are stone replicas of the original bones that minerals replaced. This box was filled with shattered, white bone. Someone had done a good job bashing them to pieces.

But the pieces were large. This hadn't been a skeleton, it had been a large bony structure, like a shoulder blade or a skull. He picked through the box and found a few very big, very reptilian teeth.

This island wasn't supposed to have any animal life on it according to Hisoka. Either a carcass washed ashore or those workers had found a very big exception to the resort's no-animals policy. This piqued his curiosity, and while the painstaking process of prepping the fossils would take a long time to get visible results, he could solve this little puzzle pretty quickly.

He wheeled the cart over to the work table and dumped the box's contents out. He sorted them by size and began to piece them together.

Six hours passed so quickly he was shocked that he'd worked through lunch, if the no-dining dining room served lunch. Working without knowing the creature one was working on made a reconstruction more difficult, but that was par for the course for a paleontologist. The fossils he dug from the ground never came with identification tags. He always warned his graduate students that the work was like putting together a puzzle without seeing the cover picture on the box, having some pieces missing, and having some incorrect pieces tossed in just to make the task interesting. The superstitious workers had done a splendid pulverizing job, which made it more of a challenge.

What the workers' tools could not break were the teeth, and they were huge. Sharpened carnivore teeth that would have looked at home in a Triassic predator's mouth. A lot of them had to be missing, but the ones he had varied in size. The smallest was still bigger than his thumb.

He had been able to reconstruct one thing, an eye socket. It measured half a foot across and the bone around it was thicker than a human shoulder blade. From the angles of that bone, the creature's field of view exceeded 120 degrees, allowing a straight ahead view for binocular attacks as well as a side view for searching out prey.

The structure was familiar, but Grant could not quite place the species the fragments resembled. What he was certain of was that the more bone he fit together, the more chills quivered up his spine. This deadly creature had to be huge, and with the bones so fresh, more of them were alive somewhere.

CHAPTER SIX

The dinner that night involved actual food.

Power had been restored, and Marie had cooked up a storm: pan seared mahi, sauteed vegetables, and fresh bread so light that Grant wished he could eat a loaf all by himself. This was the food he'd been promised when he signed up.

Everyone from the previous night was back for this meal, and all of them seemed as happy with the change of fare as Grant was.

"Marie," Grant said. "This fish is fantastic."

"Merci," she said.

"It doesn't get any fresher," Captain Wilson said. "My crew caught this fish off the *Endeavor* this morning."

"The world's most expensive fishing boat," McGinty said.

"We only catch first-class fish," Wilson said, smiling. "Hooks baited with caviar."

"I hope that you found some interesting fossils today," Hisoka said to Grant.

"I have to say," Grant said, "those were some incredible specimens. Museum quality. Where did they come from?"

"We dug them up creating the foundation for this building," McGinty said.

"Then this is an island, not an atoll," Grant said. "The volcanic activity that raised the island off the sea floor delivered some spectacular gifts."

"They were a pain in the neck, actually. Once Rothman heard about them, he made us stop work until each was cut out of the ground in one piece. Just another item outside the project scope."

"I can see how slowing things down would be frustrating, but paleontologists around the world will thank you for saving them. I know dozens who would come here just to study them."

"At the prices we plan on charging per night," Hisoka said, "I hope they can afford it."

"I saw the fossils before they were moved to the conference room," Marie said. "They looked like something out of a monster movie."

"A plesiosaur and an ichthyosaur were the big ones," Grant said. "They were the top predators of their day."

"Like killer whales?" Captain Wilson said.

"Except they were reptiles. And like alligators and turtles, and unlike fish, they still breathed air."

"And why aren't they swimming around still, like alligators and turtles?" Marie asked.

"A mass extinction occurred, called the Cretaceous–Paleogene extinction event. Something snuffed out almost all life on Earth. Perhaps an asteroid impact or volcanic activity that clouded the sky and lowered the sea temperatures several degrees."

"That would be enough to kill something that big?" Allen said.

"Aquatic animals evolve to a specific niche. You'd be surprised how a small temperature or salinity change can cause mass die offs."

"I've seen that happen," Captain Wilson said.

"Now that supposed fossil the workers smashed," Grant said, "the one in the box? That was something different. That was not a fossil. It's bone from something recently alive."

"We've been building here for months," McGinty said. "There's no animal life at all."

"It might have washed up on shore already dead," Grant said. "Some kind of predatory fish or mammal. Might be reptilian."

"We have saltwater crocodiles in the Pacific," Kaelo said. "They've been known to swim from island to island if they need a new food source. Sometimes great distances."

"This one might have underestimated the distance it was going to travel," Grant said. "Or got caught in a storm."

"If you find a live one," Marie said, "I know a great Cajun recipe for preparing the tail."

"I'll have my men keep a look out," Allen said. "We don't need any surprise animal encounters when guests start arriving."

"I'm no fan of surprise animal encounters," Grant said. "I prefer mine sixty million years dead, thank you. I can't wait to get back to those fossils tomorrow."

"Well, you won't be able to do it for long," McGinty said. "We all need to be out of the building most of the day."

"What for?"

"More work outside the project scope. We need to prep and level the concrete surfaces in the hall and rooms to put in the rest of the tile. The sanding kicks up particulates you don't want to breathe and the treatments we put on the surface afterwards aren't any healthier. I don't have enough respirators for everyone, so we'll need to take a break outside for most of the day."

That didn't sit well at all with Grant. He was ready to get some work done.

"Who wants to take a tour of the island's coast in the *Endeavor*?" Captain Wilson volunteered. "We have a new sonar rig that needs to be tested and calibrated. All of you can relax on deck while we test it out."

"Give me access to your galley and I will make us lunch," Marie said.

Grant's attitude changed. A day cruise on the Pacific with five-star food would be a nice relaxer before he started preparing the fossils. He wasn't going to be able to be in the building anyway.

"I wouldn't mind a break," Hisoka said.

"Hell, the flooring crew doesn't need me watching over their shoulder on this one," McGinty said. "I'm in."

Even Allen gave the idea an approving nod, as did Kaelo.

"Super," Captain Wilson said. "We'll set sail at 0800 from the dock. I promise a pleasant little day on the sea."

CHAPTER SEVEN

"Hold it!" Banoy shouted as he waved his hands in the air.

Danielo brought the yellow front loader to a jarring halt. He throttled back the engine and looked up the side in time to see his partner scramble down to the front tire. Banoy extracted a washed-up board with a plethora of rusty nails protruding from the end.

The two of them had been assigned to take the front loader out to the north end of the island to level and extend the beach.

"Only God can make a beach," Mr. McGinty had told them, "But only man can make it better."

They had spent the day doing just that, moving sand from one place to another and leveling the shore to better accommodate beach chairs and umbrellas. Going had been slow. Driftwood and debris that had been buried in the beach kept popping up. Twice they had to dig the loader wheels out from siltier sand. Now the sun was setting and they hadn't gotten as much done as they should have.

Banoy dragged the potential wooden spike strip off the beach and waved at Danielo. Danielo gave the kid the thumbs-up. Banoy was just a teenager, but he worked hard and was conscientious. Danielo would trade that for experience in a co-worker any day. He'd been doing work like this for thirty years and was done dealing with lazy people.

He revved the engine, dropped the bucket down and backed up. He left a smooth stripe of compacted sand behind him. He turned the loader to face the sea and nudged it forward until the bucket was over the water. He lowered it with a splash. A wave rolled more seawater into the bucket. Pouring this on the sand would compact it and make it even tighter on the next pass.

Out in the water, Danielo watched the waves roll in over what looked like rocks. But he was certain there were no rocks off this beach. The low angle of the sun made it hard to tell what was out there. He paused the loader for a closer look.

The rocky bumps seemed to move closer. He chalked that up to an optical illusion from the rolling waves. Then the bumps moved fast enough to make little wakes.

Danielo flicked on the front loader headlights. They lit up the water, and the two yellow eyes rushing toward him. He sat up in the seat in shock.

The head of a giant crocodile surfaced, almost as wide as the front loader. The croc got within a few yards of the front loader's bucket and then exploded out of the water. Its jaws opened and clamped down on the front loader's bucket. Danielo was certain the croc would crack its jaw. Instead, the bucket crunched into a U. The beast backed up and dragged the loader to the water's edge.

Banoy screamed from somewhere behind him on the beach.

Danielo revved the engine and threw the loader into reverse. The tires threw up plumes of sand and the loader crawled away from the sea. The croc did not let go and the loader pulled it out of the water up to its forelimbs. The massive size made Danielo's heart skip a beat. It had to be twice as long as his loader.

The croc bellowed and dug its feet into the sand. The loader's tires kept spinning but the machine didn't move. Then the croc dragged the loader back toward the sea.

The front tires hit the water and sent two rooster tails of silty water streaming past the croc's head on either side. Danielo pressed the already floored accelerator harder, as if somehow the engine could be coaxed to give more than its redlined rpm maximum.

The croc shook the loader and threw Danielo back and forth in his seat. His seatbelt bit into his gut and kept him from sailing out into the surf. But his foot slipped off the accelerator. The engine died. The croc yanked the loader deeper into the water.

"Jump! Jump!" Banoy shouted.

The water rose up to the bottom of Danielo's seat. He fumbled in panic at his seatbelt. It released just as the water reached his waist. He threw himself off the side of the loader and into the sea. The loader rushed by him into deeper water. A fairing slammed his shoulder and sent a bolt of pain across his shoulder blades. He screamed and his arm went numb. He rolled away from the loader and sank underwater.

He tried to swim, but his arm wouldn't move. His heavy work boots made kicking his feet feel like moving concrete blocks. He slipped deeper beneath the waves and into darkness.

Suddenly, he was at the surface in daylight. He spat out a mouthful of water and sucked in a huge gulp of air. Banoy's arm was wrapped around his chest and the kid was pulling him ashore.

They made it into shallow water. The two of them stood and then staggered out of the water and up the beach. They collapsed on the sand a few yards from the surf.

"Thank you," Danielo said.

"What the hell was that thing?" Banoy said

"I don't know."

The croc had declared victory and abandoned the front loader. The machine was almost completely underwater. Four deep ruts gouged down the beach showed where the tires had tried to claw their way out of the crocodile's grip.

"Why did it attack the loader?" Banoy said.

"If it was looking for something to eat," Danielo said, "it figured out the loader wasn't it."

"Then it's still hungry," Banoy said.

The crocodile burst from the water directly below them. In a flash, the creature raced up the sand. It rotated its head completely sideways and opened its jaws. It slammed its head into the sand with its jaws on either side of the two men.

The crocodile's humid breath reeked of rotting fish. A U of white, sharp teeth pointed at Danielo and his heart skipped a beat.

Then the jaws snapped closed. The force crushed the two men to death before either could scream.

The attack left one of Danielo's arms and one of Banoy's legs in the sand. Blood oozed from the limbs.

The crocodile backed down into the sea. Satiated, it turned to swim north back to its nest on Atoll X.

CHAPTER EIGHT

Grant stopped at the end of the dock, awestruck by the boat moored to it.

The *Endeavor* was the type of yacht only the ultra-rich owned. Over 130 feet long, it took up half the length of the dock. It shined blazing white under the tropical sun and every chromed fitting sparkled like a diamond. The windows of the main cabin were combined into one long section of smoked glass which made the white bridge deck above seem to float in the air. The stern of the boat hosted a wide-open sundeck. Grant wondered if there was a pool back there as well.

Marie walked up beside him. She shaded her eyes with one hand and looked at the yacht.

"When Captain Wilson said he did cargo runs for the island," Grant said, "I kind of pictured the boat from the original King Kong movie."

"It is nice, but I won't be impressed until I see the galley." Marie patted the fanny pack around her waist. "I had some food loaded aboard, but I'm carrying all my own spices myself. Let's hope the rest of the cutlery and pans are up to the task."

"I'm going to guess Mr. Rothman would expect five-star cuisine on a boat like this."

"You'd be surprised how common it is for people like Mr. Rothman to not know what five-star cuisine really is."

The chief of security was the next to arrive. A pistol hung on one hip and a handheld radio on the other.

Grant pointed to Allen's gun. "You know how to emphasize the 'pleasure' in pleasure cruise, don't you?"

"I'm contractually required to be armed at all times, as is everyone on my team," Allen said. "Plus, I've seen every *Jaws* movie. It pays to have some firepower out there."

The three headed to a gangplank that angled up from the dock to the taller deck of the boat. When they got to the top, Grant saw that Kaelo and McGinty were already standing on the sundeck. McGinty broke into a big smile.

"All my fears are quieted," he said. "The chef is here."

Captain Wilson stepped out of the cabin. "I think having the captain aboard might be more important."

"Hardly. Going without a captain could get us shipwrecked but with a good chef, we could survive in style until help arrived."

"Well, the crew and I can manage to get you around the island safely," Captain Wilson said. "Some of the trip will be a little slow as we calibrate the new sonar rig, but no one is in a hurry, right?"

Everyone agreed.

The captain ordered the ship readied to depart. Two crewmen pulled up the gangplank and loosened the lines securing the ship. With a muted rumble and a puff of smoke from vents in the stern, the ship came to life. Power lines and hawsers were cast off and the *Endeavor* backed away from the dock. In no time the ship was out to sea miles off the island.

The boat was exceptionally stable as it cut through the light chop. The warm breeze and the brilliant sun made Grant sigh as he leaned against the sundeck railing. Kaelo came up and stood beside him.

"Are you disappointed that you have to pause your work on your second day here?" he said.

"Yes, but I can certainly force myself to endure this level of disappointment. There are some great fossils here, so my trip will be worthwhile. Have you found any proof of past Tongan settlements so far?"

"No, and I did not expect to."

"But you said Tongans crisscrossed the Pacific. This island and atoll are relatively close to Tonga. Were they just unknown?"

"No, they were well known. My people discovered this island and what everyone calls Atoll X hundreds of years ago. We named both of them together the Forbidden Islands."

"That had to kill property values," Grant said. "Why were they forbidden?"

"That part was pretty cloudy. Stories of diseases, sharks, dangerous reefs, wild animals. But every story ended with all island visitors dying. It's probably best if I don't find any Tongan history here. It will be grim."

As they circled around the north end of the island, Atoll X could be seen on the horizon.

"I saw Atoll X from the air flying in," Grant said. "Have you been over to check it out?"

"According to Parker Rothman, that atoll is still Forbidden Island. I had to sign a statement that I understood it was a complete nature preserve and I had no access to it. He may have no problems building on this island, but he's strict as hell about making sure that atoll remains pristine. I'm on his side on that one."

"It's a great idea," Grant said. "One undisturbed atoll like that could host uncountable species of marine life and radiate biodiversity for miles around."

"There's the proof that it works," Kaelo pointed to a crewman playing out line from a huge fishing rod at the stern. "Jorgenson is doing long-line fishing. Mahi, tuna, marlins. He catches some whoppers that end up on our dinner table."

Just then the fishing line screamed as it played out from the huge reel on the rod. Jorgenson jumped at it to keep it from being pulled off the boat. Allen and McGinty rushed to his side. The crewman began adjusting the drag on the reel.

A hundred yards off the stern, a silver flash blasted out of the water. The great fish had a long spear-shaped bill. The top third of its body was a beautiful dark blue, including its dorsal fin and powerful tail. The fish had to be ten feet long. It jerked back and forth and dove back into the water.

"There's dinner!" Kaelo said. "Pacific blue marlin. Let's hope he doesn't throw the hook."

The boat went to idle to help with landing the marlin. Kaelo led Grant to the railing at the stern. They joined Allen and McGinty and the four watched the crewman wrestle with the fish. The sailor's muscles bulged with each pull of the rod that brought the marlin in closer. It leapt into the air two more times, but the hook held fast. Minutes later, the exhausted fish was just yards from the boat, the fight apparently knocked out of it.

"Soto!" Jorgenson called out. "Help me land this thing!"

Another crewman arrived with a gaffing rod to hook the fish and bring it aboard.

A huge gray fin broke the surface behind the marlin. The leading edge had a sweeping curve to it with a trailing edge that dropped straight down. Fifteen feet behind it, the tip of the tail swept back and forth through the water.

"Great white shark," Kaelo said. "He's going to want our dinner as well. Now it's a race."

Soto shouted a warning. Jorgensen reeled in line so fast it sounded like the reel was wailing in protest.

The fin disappeared.

"Looks like the shark quit," Grant said.

Then the shark burst out of the water from under the marlin. An enormous set of jaws opened incredibly wide to display rows of giant triangular teeth. They snapped shut leaving the marlin between them with the head sticking out on one side and the tail on the other. The shark's black eyes seemed to stare at the men along the stern, the way a king would look down on an unworthy rival. Then the shark dove out of sight.

Line spun off the reel and the rod bent to an impossible angle as the shark pulled the hooked marlin deep. Soto dropped his gaffing hook and whipped out a knife. He slashed at the fishing line and cut it.

The rod recoiled and whipped back and forth several times before holding still.

"Marlin is no longer on the menu," Grant said.

The water at the boat's stern churned as a struggle beneath the waves played out. A cloud of blood erupted from below. Grant figured the marlin had just met its maker.

Then the severed head of the great white rose to the surface with the marlin still clamped in its jaws. It rolled over and sank into the depths. The two crewmen looked at each other in shock.

"Whoa," McGinty said. "What the hell did we just see?"

"Kaelo," Grant said, "What would hunt a great white?"

"Killer whales have been known to. A sperm whale could if it was motivated enough."

"I didn't see any whale spouts out there," McGinty said.

Jorgenson shouted to the bridge that they'd lost the fish. The engines went back up to speed and the boat surged forward.

A call for Allen came over his radio. He plucked the unit from his belt and answered as he walked away from the group. His brow knit as he talked. Then he climbed up to the bridge and spoke to the captain. The ship turned to a more southerly heading as Allen returned to the group.

"I just got a call that two of the crew working beach refurbishment never came back last night."

McGinty looked distressed. "That was Danielo and the new kid, Banoy."

"The idiots didn't bring a radio," Allen said. "We're pretty close to where they were working. We're going to go take a look. Maybe they just had a mechanical breakdown and didn't want to hike all the way back as it got dark."

"I certainly hope so," McGinty said.

The engines ramped up to a dull roar and the boat cut a white, frothy wake from both sides of the bow.

After witnessing the inexplicable demise of the ocean's most feared predator, Grant had a bad feeling about the fate of the two overdue men.

CHAPTER NINE

The yacht soon stopped offshore. Grant didn't have to look hard to find where the two men had been working. The top of a yellow front loader's cab stuck out of the sea like a giant Tonka toy in a bathtub. Deep ruts in the sand stretched up the beach from the cab.

The captain lowered the anchor.

"This is as close as I want to get," he called down from the bridge. "Not with the sonar calibration incomplete."

"Looks like those idiots drove into the water," McGinty said. "Danielo knows better than that."

Allen had borrowed a pair of binoculars from the crew. He put them to his eyes and scanned the area.

McGinty slapped a palm against the railing. "That loader is screwed to hell now. Might as well push it in further and make it into a reef."

"The cab looks empty," Allen said.

"They're probably in the shade of those trees, waiting for someone to come drive them home."

Given the great white shark that had just stolen their lunch, Grant wondered if even the short swim from the submerged loader to the shore was safe.

Allen panned the binoculars across the beach. "No, they aren't on the beach. But there's blood up on the sand and two severed limbs."

Allen handed the binoculars to McGinty who practically gave himself a concussion planting them on his face. Allen grabbed his radio and called for a security team to head to the beach area.

McGinty gasped and then lowered the binoculars. He handed them to Grant. It seemed more like he wanted to avoid looking through them again than that he thought Grant needed a turn.

Grant's curiosity demanded he check the beach. He saw the two limbs and the massive stain of dried blood in sand around them. He reminded himself to dope-slap his curiosity later.

"What could have happened to them?" McGinty said.

"Pirates," Allen said. "They could have come ashore to kidnap them for ransom. Maybe Danielo tried to ram their boat with the loader."

Grant gave the area between the sea and the body parts a closer look. No footprints or signs of a struggle. No marks of a boat coming ashore. There wasn't any evidence to support the security chief's theory. He handed the glasses back to Allen.

"Check the beach again," Grant said. "Everything is perfectly smooth except for between the blood stain and the water. There's a big scrape in the sand there. And a yard or so to either side, the sand is churned up in regular intervals."

Grant was afraid to say they looked like huge footprints. He didn't want everyone to think he was letting his imagination run wild. More than that, he didn't want to admit to himself that it might be. But the giant broken skull in the box came from something.

"Are you a detective now?" Kaelo said.

"Only when solving mysteries millions of years old," Grant said. "I've learned to look for signs like this in fossilized stone."

"We should go in and take a look," Allen said. "My team is on their way in an ATV but that will take over an hour."

"You can paddle one of the inflatable boats in." The captain turned to the crewman at the stern who'd been manning the fishing rod. "Jorgensen, break out an inflatable from the aft locker."

Jorgenson went to a locker on the starboard side. He threw it open and pulled out a block of gray rubber. Everyone stepped back and Jorgensen pulled a cord at the top of the raft. Compressed air whooshed and the cube unrolled and unfolded into a big raft with a pointed bow. Jorgensen extracted four paddles from the locker.

"Kaelo," Allen said, "give me a hand paddling this thing to shore, will you?"

"I'm going as well," McGinty said. "Those were my men."

Something buzzed overhead. Grant looked up to see a medium-sized four-rotor drone circling the boat. Allen let fly a slew of curses.

"I didn't know island security had a drone," Captain Wilson said.

"We don't," Allen answered. "But pirates usually do."

CHAPTER TEN

Grant's pulse quickened as he dashed for the other side of the boat. He looked out to sea.

"Any pirates out there?" Allen said.

"Honestly," Grant said, "other than a tall ship flying the Jolly Roger, I don't know what a pirate ship looks like."

"Right now," Allen said, "anything you see afloat is a pirate ship."

Allen keyed the mic on his radio and called the security office. All he got in response was static.

"Captain, call the resort on your radio," he shouted up to the bridge.

The captain disappeared and then reappeared. "I can't get through."

"That drone is scrambling our radio signals," Allen said.

"I'm going to guess that's bad," Grant said.

"Depends on how much you like being kidnapped."

"I can say from experience that I don't enjoy it." He could have added that he didn't know anyone with the ability or the inclination to pay a ransom to set him free.

"Captain, you need to get us out of here!" Allen shouted.

The captain flashed a thumbs-up and disappeared again. At the bow, the anchor line began to winch up. The engines roared to life and the sea at the stern churned into a frothy boil. The boat began to move forward.

From across the water came the sound of a thundering engine. An eighteen-foot-long open skiff with two huge outboard motors came skimming into view. A group of men sat in the bow and one man stood at the center controls.

"Pirates ahoy," Grant said.

"That's a pretty small boat this far out on the ocean," McGinty said.

"There's a bigger mothership nearby, trust me," Allen said.

Grant pulled a sport strap from his pocket and quickly strapped his glasses tight to his head.

"You always carry that with you?" McGinty said.

"It has really come in handy the last few years."

Allen climbed the steps to the bridge as the *Endeavor* started a canted right-hand turn. Grant and the others followed Allen. The drone continued to cross back and forth over the boat.

The *Endeavor* accelerated, but the skiff continued to close the gap.

"Can't we go faster?" McGinty said.

"It's a big ship to get moving," the captain said. "But even at full speed, we are no match for that light a boat."

The skiff closed to a distance where Grant could make out details, and they weren't reassuring. Four men in a hodgepodge of olive drab and camouflage clothing sat in the bow cradling AK-47 rifles. The taller man at the controls wore a backwards baseball cap and oversized aviator sunglasses.

A fifth sat further back with something in his lap, probably the drone controller. The drone flew back to the skiff and that man caught it in his hand.

Kaelo had ended up with the binoculars and checked out the skiff. "Filipinos. The insurgents from the islands are finding piracy a great way to finance their operations. Their brutality is legendary."

"So is my aversion to pain," Grant said.

Marie came out of the cabin onto the sundeck and called up to the bridge. "I'm trying to cook down here. What are you people doing?"

"Trying not to get boarded." Grant pointed across the sea to the skiff.

Marie saw the boat and her face went white. She rushed back into the cabin.

"What is your crew armed with?" Allen said.

"Plastic stirrers and cocktail napkins," the captain said. "We're a private yacht. And I didn't even bring the full crew for this little trip around the island."

The yacht headed straight north away from the island and toward Atoll X.

"Why are we heading away from the resort and all our well-armed security men?" Grant said.

"Sonar isn't reliable and I can't risk guessing where the local reefs are. We'll need to make a wider swing before we can get back around."

Now the *Endeavor* was cruising, slicing through the sea and sending white spray up either side of the bow. But the captain had foretold the outcome correctly. The skiff still closed on them.

Sweat broke out across Grant's forehead. This was supposed to be a boat ride, not an evil reimagining of *Treasure Island*. He looked around and tried to think what he could use to defend himself from the pirates. All he could come up with was hitting them with one of the life rings on the sundeck.

The skiff broke to starboard and crossed the Endeavor's wake. That put it between the ship and the island. The captain turned the boat on a course more aimed at Atoll X.

"They're putting themselves between the island and us," he said. "Forcing us further out. If they can board us in deep enough water, they'll bring the mother ship in and try to not only kidnap us, but seize the ship."

As if to emphasize that point, one of the men in the skiff sent a spray of bullets in the *Endeavor's* direction.

"Tell me Parker Rothman was rich enough to buy a bulletproof boat," Grant said.

"Does this look like a battleship?" the captain said.

An alarm sounded by the captain. The circular sonar screen to his right flashed over to solid green.

"Damn it," he said. "Sonar's completely winked out. We're sailing ahead full speed and blind through uncharted reefs. We hit one and we'll tear the bottom out of this boat."

Another round of gunfire came from the skiff. Windows along the starboard side shattered. Grant ducked behind the bulkhead.

"Just keep running too fast for them to board us," Allen said. "Get us back near the resort, my men will be in position to take that skiff out."

Grant rose to a crouch and looked over the bow. Atoll X was coming up fast. At a thousand yards out, the sugary beach and swaying palms were easy to make out. Blue waves rolled ashore and created explosions of white as they hit the sand.

"Where's a fort full of cannons when you need one?" Grant said.

The skiff captain apparently decided the *Endeavor* had gone far enough. He poured on the power and came up alongside the boat at about fifty feet away. These pirates looked even more unsavory closer up; unshaven, tattooed, weathered. The one at the wheel had a thick, ropy scar running down his left cheek. Stained machetes lay on the skiff's deck. Grant didn't want to think about what they might be stained with. The skiff skipper shouted something up to the bridge in a language Grant did not understand.

"He wants us to cut the engines," Kaelo said.

"Tell him we'll pass on that," Grant said.

One of the men leveled a rifle at the bridge. Grant dropped to one knee. The AK-47 opened up and bullets ripped into the overhead and the controls. Splinters rained down in all directions. Dials in the cockpit exploded in showers of sparks and glass. Hot embers landed on Grant's scalp and he brushed at them in a flailing panic.

Allen drew his pistol and returned fire. The skiff's engines throttled up and the craft veered away. Perhaps the skipper hadn't planned on anyone on this fancy yacht having firearms.

"It's all fun and games until someone shoots back," Grant said.

From deep within the ship came the sound of shattering fiberglass and snapping wood. An alarm blared and red lights on the cockpit console lit up.

Suddenly, the boat came to a lurching halt. Everyone on the bridge was thrown forward into the bulkhead. Grant slammed head-first into a fire extinguisher on the wall. The clanging noise his skull made would have been hilarious if it hadn't hurt like hell.

Grant pulled himself to his feet. The ship began a roll to the left.

"We hit a reef." Captain Wilson looked over at the red alarm lights. "The hull is compromised in three compartments. Pumps are on."

"They'll get us back afloat?" McGinty said.

"No. They'll just let us sink slower."

"First thing when I get home," Grant said, "I'm firing my agent."

Off to the left, the pirate skiff made a wide circle and started a slow approach to the yacht. One of the men readied a grappling hook to toss up on the deck.

"I'm not going to be able to hold them off with this," Allen said, waving his pistol.

Just as the pirate readied to let the grappling hook fly, a dark shape rose from the depths. At least thirty feet long, it was shaped like a broad cigar, but any detail was impossible to make out with all the sediment kicked up in the water. It slammed into the bottom of the skiff, drove it up to expose its barnacled hull, and then drove it sideways out away from the yacht. The pirates cried out, dropped their weapons, and hung on to keep from being thrown overboard.

The drone pilot in the stern was not as lucky. He toppled over the side. The boat sucked him under and back into the propellers. The engines bogged down under the stress and a spray of blood and flesh exploded up from the stern. Then the engines died.

The skiff settled in the water to the sound of something hard and scaly scraping against the fiberglass hull. The black shape dove down into the water.

The remaining men in the boat panicked. One grabbed an AK and began spraying the water on all sides with bullets until the gun clicked empty. The scarred skipper went to the wheel and tried to restart the engines. On the second try they turned over. He gunned the throttle and the stern dug in deep. A spin of the wheel swung the bow away from the *Endeavor*, and the pirates beat a hasty retreat. The gunner slammed another magazine into his AK and shot up the sea to the stern as they roared away.

"Not that I want to look a gift horse in the mouth," McGinty said, "but what the hell was that?"

"I'm going to guess the same thing that chomped that great white," Grant said. "And nothing I ever want to see again."

The ship lurched left and sank deeper into the water. All the lights in the cockpit went dark.

"She's going down," Captain Wilson said. "There's no stopping it."

"The raft," Kaleo said. "We can take it to the atoll."

"That's a long paddle," the captain said. "And the same reef that sank us might tear the bottom out of a raft even faster."

"We can't stay here." Kaelo pointed off the side of the boat. Where the skiff engines had pureed the pirate, two shark fins circled in the water.

Jorgenson stood beside Marie, gripping the railing at the stern. The captain called down to him to break out a second raft.

"Everyone get down to the sundeck," the captain said. "Get in one of the rafts and start for shore. I need to check on the crew and get them out of here."

Captain Wilson descended a set of steps into the main cabin. The rest of them scrambled down the steps to the sundeck. Grant gave the rising water and the raft equally uncomfortable looks.

"Can't you swim?" McGinty said.

"I can. I just had a bad experience with water as a kid."

"When?"

"Every encounter between age three and eighteen."

Allen was the first one to make it to the inflated raft. Jorgensen was just pulling the inflation handle on the second one. Allen and Kaelo brought the raft to the low side of the yacht. It wasn't going to take much to launch it. Water already lapped at the bottom of the railing.

They heaved it into the rising water. Grant motioned for Marie to climb in.

"After you," he said.

"Is that gallantry?" Marie asked.

"No, I'm just prioritizing the person who can best feed us." He pointed to her fanny pack. "You still have your spices."

Marie looked taken off guard and put a hand on her pack. "Yes, I guess I do."

She hopped in like a nimble little pixie. Grant followed her with a clumsy tumble that shipped a half gallon of water into the raft. McGinty and Kaelo followed. Kaelo held the paddles.

Allen spun the raft around until the bow pointed to Atoll X. By now the rising water lapped against his knees. He pulled himself aboard, then kicked the raft away from the boat with his feet.

Kaelo and McGinty paddled the raft a short distance from the boat. The *Endeavor* didn't have long. The passage to the main cabin was now awash. The captain emerged, supporting a dazed-looking Soto. Bright blood coated the man's left leg.

The remaining raft floated on the flooded sundeck. Jorgenson pushed it over to the captain and Soto. They both helped Soto into the raft, then climbed in after him, and began to paddle in pursuit of the first raft.

When they were twenty yards from the yacht, a crunching sound came from under the sea. Metal moaned and shockwaves made the water tremble so hard Grant had to grip the side of the raft. Then the stern of the boat dipped beneath the waves. The bow rose and then the entire ship slid down the reef with a chilling, scraping noise and disappeared. Bubbles and foam boiled up from the spot where the ship had been, and then the waves washed all that away, as if nothing had ever been there.

Grant watched in shock. For something so huge to be gone so quickly was almost unbelievable. One of Kaelo's paddles sent a slap of water onto his face and snapped him out of it. Both rafts headed for the beach.

Ahead lay the sand and surf of Atoll X. There wouldn't be any people on the deserted atoll to make their situation any better. And based on what he'd just seen attack the pirate skiff, he had a bad feeling whatever creatures might inhabit the atoll were going to make everything worse.

CHAPTER ELEVEN

Grant wished the raft would move faster. The sooner he got out of the water and away from whatever they'd seen hit that skiff, the better he'd feel. In his terror he almost started hand paddling over the side, but that wouldn't have made the raft any quicker and would have put his panic on display for everyone. There were some things better kept to himself.

The raft closed on the atoll. With a few yards left to go, the little boat caught a wave and surfed all the way up onto the beach. The five of them jumped out.

"Hello dry land!" Grant said. "I'd kiss the ground, but I don't know where it's been."

"We aren't out of the woods yet," Allen said. "We can't assume the pirates gave up. Grab the raft and everyone get up into the tree line."

The group grabbed the edges of the raft and pulled it up into the trees. As they did, the second raft with the captain and the two crewmen nosed ashore. Captain Wilson and Jorgenson helped Soto out of the raft. Soto grimaced and moaned with every movement. Grant, McGinty, and Allen went down to meet them.

"How badly is he hurt?" Allen said.

"He won't be running marathons," Wilson said. "I think it's broken, but not a compound fracture."

"Get him up someplace dry."

Wilson and Jorgenson helped Soto to a spot above the high tide line along the beach. Marie joined them and knelt beside Soto.

Allen, McGinty, and Grant dragged the second raft up out of the water. One of the compartments on the raft had partially deflated. As he noticed that, so did Grant's spirits. The more ways they had off this atoll, the happier he would be.

Wilson joined them by the rafts. "There were three other crewmen trapped below decks. I...I couldn't get to them."

Allen took his radio from his belt and checked it. It was dead. Water dripped out of the bottom of the case. He cursed and threw it on the ground.

Back at the trees, Kaelo pulled a large collapsible knife from his pocket and snapped it open. The wide blade was almost five inches long and ended in a sharp point. He slashed a low-hanging palm frond free and took it down to the beach. Kaelo swept the sand between the sea and the raft with the branch until all traces of their arrival had been erased.

"That was smart," Grant said.

"I may have done some trespassing in my youth," Kaelo said. "I know a few tricks to help stay hidden."

"Now what do we do?" McGinty said

"I wasn't able to send out a distress signal," Wilson said. "No one knows we sank or where we are."

"There's no human presence on this atoll," Allen said. "Rothman has left it completely alone. Not even a wildlife camera. But when my people realize they've lost contact with the *Endeavor*, they'll start a search in our skiff."

"Unless they're using a submarine," Grant said, "they won't find the yacht."

"And they'll search all around the island before they check out the atoll," Kaelo said. "We're not supposed to be here."

"If all of you are trying to make me feel hopeful," Grant said, "you're doing a lousy job."

"Our best bet," McGinty said, "is to pull this raft up with us and stay hidden in the trees in case the pirates return. If rescuers arrive first, we can run out on the beach and get their attention."

Grant's stomach rumbled. "The least the pirates could have done was attack after lunch."

"Mr. McGinty's right," Allen said. "We'll sit tight here. Stay in the shade to minimize dehydration. Someone will come for us."

Out past the waves, two large, black-green bumps surfaced in the water.

Grant's heart began to thud in his chest. He tapped Allen on the shoulder and pointed to the water. "What if some*thing* comes for us first?"

Eyelids opened to reveal two bright, yellow eyes. A few feet closer to shore, bumpy nostrils broke the surface, followed by the outline of an entire snout. Then a ridge of back armor rose out of the sea. A long tail swished in the water behind it. This was the biggest crocodile Grant had ever seen, at least thirty feet long.

Everyone but Soto jumped to their feet. Marie screamed. Grant followed suit.

The pieces came together and he realized the creature whose bones had been in the box back at the resort. A crocodile, but one so big he couldn't recognize it. Until now.

Allen drew his pistol.

Grant remembered how thick the bone in the crocodile skull had been. "Good luck with that."

The croc stared at them.

"Thank God we got away from the water," McGinty said.

Kaelo stepped back farther up the beach. "We still aren't safe. You have no idea how fast—"

The croc blasted out of the sea in a blur of dark green leather and white water. It charged at them over the raft. The huge claws on its fore feet tore holes in the raft's compartments and compressed air escaped in a chorus of booms.

Adrenaline blasted Grant into panicked flight. He spun around to see the entire group sprinting for the trees. He ran to join them.

Soto couldn't. He cried out and tried to stand. He never made it. The croc was on him in a flash, jaws wide open.

"Soto!" Jorgenson shouted out.

With a quick sideways snap, Soto disappeared within its jaws. The croc's rear foot had impaled the raft. The monster turned and retreated to the sea, dragging the deflated rubber raft with it. The creature disappeared into the surf.

Jorgenson started to run for the water. Wilson grabbed his shoulders and held him back.

"He's gone," Wilson said.

The group reassembled at the spot where Soto was taken. A trail of blood ran through the sand to the sea. The croc had churned into a mess the sand Kaelo had just manicured. There was no sign of the creature in the water. Small waves lapped the shore as if that horrific act of violence had just been an aberration in a perpetually idyllic world.

Marie touched Wilson's arm. "I'm so sorry."

Tears welled in Wilson's eyes. "He was a good man."

"Those marks in the sand are the same ones made on Nirvana Island," Kaelo said. "Those workers weren't taken by pirates."

"I'll bet they wish they had been," Grant said.

"And that thing attacked the pirate boat," McGinty said.

"Why would it save us," Marie said, "only to turn around and attack us?"

"Maybe it wasn't saving us," Grant said. "It was more the equivalent of keeping the pirates from raiding its refrigerator."

"Maybe it won't come back," McGinty said.

"You won't have just one giant crocodile on an atoll," Grant said. "It's not like a Godzilla movie. In real life, if there's one, there's a whole population of them. There's a skull from one back at the resort."

"Someone's going to pay for not warning my crew about these things," McGinty said.

"I guarantee no one knew about giant crocodiles," Allen said, "because I didn't."

"The damn things killed two of my men back on Nirvana Island," McGinty said. "Don't tell me no one knew these things were here."

"My men and I have been on the island for months," Allen said, "even before construction started. There were no signs of giant crocodiles."

"I don't believe you."

"I do," Grant said. "Before construction, the uninhabited island had no food sources for them, no reason for a crocodile to swim over there. But people arrived, a nice easy-to-digest meal. Now that they know, the crocs will be back again."

"And they'll be back here as well," Kaelo said. "We need to get away from the beach."

"But then how will we get rescued if we're in the jungle?" Marie said. "No one will even know we're here."

"We'll leave a marker on the beach," Allen said. "That will tell my men we're here. Finding us won't be difficult after that. The atoll isn't that big. We'll need to take our chances that the pirates won't want to tangle with that croc again. Gather up some of these fallen palm branches."

The group began to scour the area and collected brown, dried branches from the ground. Jorgenson just stared at the ground, as if dazed. Wilson went to his side.

"C'mon, Jorgenson. We need to get to work."

"Soto is gone," Jorgensen said. "I mean gone! Pirates were bad enough, drowning all the men below decks. But then that monster just…attacked…"

"Hang in there. We'll get rescued."

"Captain, I'm no fighter. I didn't join the Navy, I signed up to crew a rich dude's yacht. None of this was in my contract."

Wilson scooped a palm branch from the ground and pressed it against Jorgenson's chest. "Get moving on gathering these palms or you won't get rescued to get out of your contract."

Jorgenson took the leaf and began a slow search for more. The rest gathered an armload each. They brought them to the beach.

"Think there's enough space to spell SEND FOOD?" Grant said.

"Just arrange them in an arrow pointing inland," Allen said. "My people will know it's a message from me that we're here."

They laid out the fronds in a thick, wide arrow. It stood out in stark relief against the white sand.

"Well, you can't miss that," Marie said.

"For now," McGinty said. "When the tide comes in, the sea will wash most of it away."

"Thanks for that cheerful thought," Grant said. "You are officially banned from being the cruise's morale officer."

"That was no normal crocodile," McGinty said. "You're the scientist, Grant. What exactly was that thing in the water?"

"That crocodile looked like *Kaprosuchus*," Grant said. "Sometimes called a boar croc. It was estimated from the few fossils found that it could grow to twenty feet long. Looks like estimates were short by ten feet. The last one walked the Earth millions of years ago."

"How does something like that still exist?" McGinty said. "It's the 21st century for God's sake."

"The world may have changed a lot since then, but this equatorial area hasn't. The waters around the atoll are full of prey and devoid of predators. Isolated from mankind, what's to keep a population of crocs from continuing on here?"

"Well, I wish something had," McGinty said.

"Let's get off the beach," Allen said. "We need shade and to see if we can find any water."

Marie turned to Grant. "Lucky you. This is the paleontological discovery of a lifetime."

Just once, Grant thought, *I'd like to go out of town and NOT make the paleontological discovery of a lifetime.*

CHAPTER TWELVE

Seven months ago.

Petra Fuchs felt filthy.

She'd taken as hot a shower as her crummy apartment's water heater would allow and scrubbed twice with soap so strong it nearly peeled off her skin, but she still felt the grit of coal dust on her body. She hadn't counted on this side effect of working at the mine in Rhineland. This was one of the sacrifices she made for her environmentalist cause, and the most ironic.

She combed out her short hair again in front of the bathroom mirror. Coal dust wouldn't show against its dark color, but she could see it as it snowed down into the sink. She checked her face in the mirror. The mine work, and life in general, was taking a toll. She thought she looked ten years older than her actual age of thirty-eight.

A knock sounded at her door. She wasn't expecting anyone. She was never expecting anyone. She walked over and checked through the peephole. A man stood back against the wall, as if consciously making sure Petra could take him all in. He wore a relatively new set of jeans and a sharp leather jacket over a black turtleneck. He ran his fingers through his blond hair. Whoever he was, he had more money than she'd seen in a long time.

"What do you want?" she said.

"My name is Klaus. I'm a job recruiter."

Petra had never been recruited for a job, only rejected. "You have the wrong apartment."

"No, Petra, I have the right apartment." To prove his point, he spouted off a list of details like her date and place of birth and several personal items. "I have an offer for you."

Petra was equal parts wary and intrigued. She stepped back into the kitchen, and pulled an automatic pistol from one of the drawers. She tucked it into the small of her back and draped her shirt over the butt. Then she let the man in.

"You can stay there by the door," she said. "Let me hear what you have to say."

The man leaned back against the door. "I have to admit, finding out you were working in a coal mine made me laugh."

"I'm the one doing it, and I don't find it funny at all."

"It's ironic. An environmentalist like you helping a company pull chunks of future carbon emissions out of the ground."

"I had to swallow my pride so I could swallow some food."

"Nothing causes more indigestion than swallowed pride," Klaus said. "You also had to do that when the Sierra Club booted you out, didn't you?"

The depth of knowledge this man had about her was starting to get scary. "How do you know about that?"

"There's an informal grapevine through the environmental community. Word gets around. Seems you were a little too extreme for those people."

Those were exactly the words the Sierra Club officials had used when they found out she'd set fire to a power substation that serviced an oil refinery.

"Something had to be done," Petra said. "No one fears a dog that is all bark and never bites."

"They just couldn't understand your level of commitment. I mean, your parents were killed in that explosion from a faulty natural gas pipeline. Some people talk about future suffering from global warming, but fossil fuel companies have already made you suffer. Well, I represent a group who agrees with you completely. Green Warriors."

Petra's eyes went wide. If some environmental groups could be considered on the radical fringe of the movement, Green Warriors was at the tip of that fringe. Terrorism wasn't their last resort; it was the first action they took.

Klaus flashed Petra a knowing smile. "No one committed enough to set fire to a substation would ever swallow enough pride to work in a coal mine. I think you had an ulterior motive."

"It wasn't a love of coal dust."

"Hardly. Your crude attempt to disable the power station failed. Gasoline and a lighter were not enough. You learned from that and knew that dramatic change would require more dramatic means."

Petra was shocked by the man's insight.

"So," he continued, "why would you work here? Access to explosives, and the opportunity to learn how to make them work. The next time you'd make an attack on the carbon industry, it was going to be a success."

Petra smiled. "And the beauty of it would be that the carbon industry taught me what I needed to know."

"Here's your chance to make the difference you've always wanted to." Klaus handed her a piece of paper with an address on it. "Be here at 11PM tonight. Wait in the office. At 11:01, the offer is withdrawn if you aren't there."

The man left the apartment before Petra could ask any of the dozen questions she had at the tip of her tongue. She looked at the address. The location was deep in an industrial section of the city.

Petra figured that she had nothing to lose, and potentially a lot to gain.

The next night, she sat in a folding chair in what had once been the office in an unused warehouse. The previous tenants had left behind everything that wasn't worth moving, including this chair and an industrial-quality metal desk with a savage dent in the front panel. Half the bulbs in the overhead fluorescent light were dead. A faded road map of Germany hung canted on one wall. The air stank of rat urine and mildew.

She wondered if the Green Warriors actually rented this dump, or if they were just squatting in it and running off hijacked electricity. She guessed the latter. Violent eco-terrorist organizations weren't much on setting up storefronts and distribution centers.

A man her age entered the office. He had his hair shaved down to almost nothing and what was left was died purple. A gold nose ring hung from his septum. A tattooed dragon's head ran across his neck like an inked scarf.

He was the first person Petra had seen since she'd entered the building. He didn't look like he had the gravitas to manage the kind of opportunity she'd been promised.

"Petra Fuchs?" he said.

"Yes. Who are you?"

"No one whose name you need to know. The word is you're the kind of person who isn't afraid to get her hands dirty. Is that true?"

"For the right cause," Petra said.

"You're in the right place," he said. "We're out to save the planet. Mankind needs to get the hell out of the way and let nature take back over. We're ready to take a big step toward making that happen. You'll need to travel far, and you might not make it back."

Petra shrugged. "If the worst happens, there's no family to mourn for me on this end, nothing special I'd be leaving behind."

"Excellent." The man sat on the edge of the desk and leaned closer to Petra. "There's a place in the Pacific we call Atoll X. It's owned by billionaire bastard Parker Rothman. He claims he's setting it aside as a private preserve where nature can flourish. In reality, we think he's full of crap. He's building a resort on the nearby island that will probably have cruise ships docking at it the first week it opens, dumping all their waste into the area."

"The top one-percent building a vacation resort for the top one-percent," Petra said, "at the expense of the planet."

"And there's no way Atoll X doesn't have something going on there as well. Our sources inside the oil industry say that parts of an oil drilling rig were delivered there, bought through a series of shell companies that trace back to Rothman. The world doesn't need another oil well, and it sure as hell doesn't need it on a pristine Pacific atoll. You will lead three others on a mission there."

"You want me to go in and expose that construction?"

"You have a much bigger objective, and a very special way to get there to do it." The man took a folder out from the drawer of his desk. "I'm happy to credit the drug cartels for the amazing boat you'll be taking to the atoll."

He took a photograph from the folder and handed it to Petra. The picture was of what looked like a miniature submarine in a cradle on dry land. It measured about fifty-feet long, with a small conning tower wrapped in windows. The picture's background looked like a rainforest instead of a shipyard.

"A submarine?" Petra said.

"It's a semi-submersible, made of fiberglass. It runs with decks awash just under the waves. The pilot stands inside that cupola and steers looking out those windows."

Petra worried that this tube could be a homemade deep-sea coffin. "That thing is safe?"

"Would drug kingpins stuff millions of dollars of cocaine in one if they sank all the time?" The man took the picture back from Petra. "We've watched other environmental organizations have their conventional ships impounded by authorities, stopping protests that don't accomplish anything anyway. Green Warriors plan on doing more than protesting, and needed something stealthier than a converted fishing boat. The black market offered this."

"It looks small."

"The boat is supposed to carry fifteen tons of narcotics. Instead, we'll load it with you and three armed activists. The boat can be run right up to the beach, and then everyone gets out. Needless to say, our intelligence so far about what's happening on the atoll is spotty. But by the time you get there, you'll have plenty. You need to put an end to whatever Rothman is up to."

"You expect four people from the submarine to do that?"

"Four people and enough explosives to make a crater worthy of the moon. If you think your new-found explosives expertise is up for it."

"It sure is." Petra smiled. This was exactly the kind of chaos she wanted to be part of.

"We need you to stop Rothman. By any means necessary."

CHAPTER THIRTEEN

Present Day

Atoll X was souring Grant on the whole tropical paradise sales pitch. The atoll's grass slashed at his ankles with sharpened edges. Palm fronds did the same every time he tried to move one out of the way. And the humidity made him want to nominate the inventor of air conditioning for sainthood.

Sweat had long ago turned his shirt into a sopping mess. Visions of heat stroke, muscle cramps, and heart palpitations created a parade of impending doom marching through his consciousness. He'd sworn it before, but this time he meant it. When he got back home, he was getting in shape.

The group broke out of dense vegetation and into a grassy clearing. They stopped for a break. Seven palm trees grew near the middle, heavy with coconuts.

Grant squinted up at the blinding sun. "Thank God. We're finally out of that annoying shade."

McGinty wiped sweat from his brow. "This heat's a killer."

"Big problem," Allen said. "We're not going to find fresh water on this atoll."

"We don't need to." Marie pointed up at the coconuts in the palms. "We have plenty to drink right over our heads."

"I thought that coconut water was some made-up faddish drink," Grant said.

"She's right," Kaelo said. "We just have to go up and get them."

The group went to the base of one tree. Grant looked up at the coconuts. The tree had to be thirty feet tall.

"I think I'll wait for them to naturally fall," Grant said. He tried to shake the trunk of the palm tree. It didn't move. "See, I just loosened them up."

"It isn't hard," Kaelo said. "I've picked coconuts from trees since I was a boy."

"As a boy," Grant said, "I took coconut crème pie out of the refrigerator."

Kaelo pulled off his shirt and exposed a disgustingly well-muscled chest with a spiraling design tattooed over one pectoral muscle. He went to the palm tree and kind of hugged it. He grabbed the shirt with both hands and twisted it until it was a tight little spiral. With a flick of his feet, he sent his sandals flying off into the sand. He pulled his shirt tight against the trunk.

Then Kaelo ran up the tree. Or at least it looked that way to Grant. His bare feet dashed up the rough palm's bark in perfect sync with him pulling tight his shirt, and then flipping it up higher on the tree. Kaelo made the task look effortless.

He stopped at the top of the tree and wrapped an arm around the trunk. With his free hand, he pulled out his knife and flicked it open. He cut away at the foliage. One by one, the three coconuts fell into Marie's waiting arms.

Kaelo climbed halfway down the tree, then dropped to the ground.

"It's easy," he said to Grant.

"Not as easy as buying shredded coconut at the supermarket," Grant said. "I'll stay down here on the receiving end."

Kaelo climbed another tree. Allen took off his belt and after one failed attempt, got the hang of it, and scaled another tree himself. They sent coconuts dropping down to Jorgenson and Marie. They tossed them to Grant, Wilson, and McGinty, who made a central pile.

Palm fronds rustled past the clearing's edge. Grant whiffed the unwelcome scent of algae and dead fish.

"Crocodile!" Allen shouted from up in the tree. He took his belt ends in one hand and pointed to the west edge of the clearing. "Everyone climb!"

The snout of a giant crocodile poked out from between some ferns. Grant's pulse broke into a sprint.

He wished his body was up for doing the same. But he'd seen those crocs run and all he'd do is delay for seconds the beast's meal of Grant tartare.

Allen reached down and grabbed Marie's hand. He helped her climb up the tree after him. The captain and McGinty already had their belts off and were climbing palms of their own.

Options flashed through Grant's mind. His belt was all that kept his shorts from dropping down to his ankles. If he used that to help his arms climb, his shorts would handcuff his feet together. And that's discounting the public humiliation of being up a tree in his boxer shorts.

To his left, Jorgenson began to shinny up the tree with his arms and legs wrapped around it. He scaled the tree like a bear. That process looked doable.

Grant lumbered to the nearest palm and jumped. He'd envisioned vaulting halfway up the tree. He actually started a foot higher than if he'd jumped from a standstill. He wrapped the tree with his arms and legs and began to climb. He moved like a pear-shaped inchworm, reaching up with his arms, then following with his legs. His rise could be measured in inches.

At the clearing's edge, the crocodile emerged from the brush. It was a third shorter than the one they'd encountered on the beach, but that still made it over twenty feet long and very wide. The teeth protruding from its upper and lower jaws didn't look any less deadly. The beast opened its jaws and hissed. The inside of its mouth was blood red.

Grant's bladder suddenly felt ready to burst. He kept climbing. Rough bristles coated the palm tree's bark and scraped at Grant's skin, even through his wet shirt. His arms began to tire almost immediately.

The crocodile charged. Jorgenson was in the palm nearest the croc and the reptile targeted his tree. In a flash, the croc was at the base of the tree and then looked up at its retreating prey. With the distance gauged, the croc rose up on its back legs and tail, then leapt up the tree.

It landed with its jaws wide open around the lower half of Jorgenson's body. He cried out and the croc's mouth snapped shut around Jorgensen and the tree. Blood sprayed from the corner of the croc's mouth. The crewman went mercifully silent and his arms went limp.

The croc dropped back to the ground, pulling the palm tree with it. The trunk bent over until it could take no more, and then it exploded with a mighty crack. With a sideways snap of its head, the croc tossed aside the broken palm tree and Jorgensen's mangled body.

At the sight of the dead crewman, Grant had to fight back vomiting. He continued his climb, with burning leg muscles now joining his arms in rebellion against this life-saving workout.

The croc uttered a rumbling growl and turned to the next closest tree, Grant's.

As a man who studied animal behavior for a living, Grant knew this development was bad. If the creature hadn't hunted Jorgensen for food, that meant it had attacked to defend its territory, and it wasn't going to stop until every invader was dead.

He tried to climb faster. The bark scraped his inner arms raw. The croc made a more measured approach to Grant's tree, as if knowing this chubby prey would never get away. It stopped at the bottom of the tree and eyed Grant. He wasn't even as far up the tree as Jorgenson had been.

A pistol shot cracked. The croc flinched and redirected its gaze to another palm. Allen clung near the top of that tree, with his pistol aimed at the croc. Marie was wrapped around the trunk just above him.

The pistol's bullet didn't seem to have pierced the croc's hide, and Grant thought it responded to the gunshot more out of curiosity about the sound than anything. Unimpressed, the croc turned back to Grant.

But Allen had bought Grant a little time, just enough to crawl up higher than Jorgenson had been, hopefully out of reach of the croc's jumping range.

The croc cocked its head and assessed Grant. Grant felt his legs go weak under the creature's yellow gaze. The croc crouched and jumped.

It hit the tree and Grant held on for his life. The trunk shook hard. A coconut broke free and bashed into Grant's shoulder on its way to the ground. The croc's jaws then slammed shut inches from Grant's feet. The creature slid off the trunk and crashed back to the ground on its side. It looked up at Grant and hissed.

Grant sighed with relief. He hadn't made it by much, but he'd made it, out of reach of the croc's leap. The others were higher up than he was, so everyone was going to make it. All they had to do was wait this big boy out.

The croc didn't admit defeat. It rolled back on its belly and circled back to the base of Grant's tree.

"Seriously?" Grant said. "I am all fat and gristle. You don't want to eat this."

The croc lay the underside of its jaw against the palm tree's base. And then, rising on its hind legs, it pushed a third of its body up along the tree trunk. The great palm began to lean.

Grant shimmied up a bit higher. But his arms and legs were done with all this exercise. His muscles began to quiver.

The croc pushed itself higher. Its belly scraped the bark off the tree as its full chest rested against the trunk. The tree bent to a horrific angle. Palms were built to sway in hurricane-force winds, but Grant knew this had to be asking too much of it. The trunk was doomed to break.

The croc pushed itself up again. Its hind legs extended and it laid most of its belly against the tree. The trunk drooped closer to the ground.

Grant's grip slipped. He rolled inverted and now hung underneath the palm. He clamped a hand around each of his wrists and locked his ankles together. One of his shoes popped off his foot and fluttered down to the ground. He was only ten feet up at this point. The drop wouldn't kill him, but the crocodile sure would.

The trunk let out a low moan as the fibers around the base began to crack.

CHAPTER FOURTEEN

A ferocious bellow swept across the clearing. The climbing croc paused and turned its head in that direction.

Another croc charged toward the palm tree grove. This reptile was much larger than the one trying to kill Grant. Its huge feet dug divots in the earth. Jagged teeth sparkled from its open maw. The new monster ignored all the people clinging to trees, and headed straight for the other croc.

The small croc hissed and jumped off the palm to face down the intruder.

The palm shot back up. Grant felt like he was being launched by a catapult. He closed his eyes and clamped the trunk in a full-body death grip.

The tree hit vertical, but the extra weight of Grant at the top sent it continuing forward. It hit its maximum rebound and tried one more time to throw Grant across the clearing. Searing shoulder pain begged him to let go, but blind panic talked him out of it. Then like a bucking bronco, the tree continued a few more diminishing swings until it stopped, pointing skyward. Grant opened his eyes to a world spinning in a circle. He threw up all over his hands.

Below him, the giant croc lunged at the smaller one. The smaller one stood its ground in the kind of naïve bravado a younger male often shows in its first attempt to sever an alpha's dominance.

The big croc hit the smaller one in the shoulder with its snout and drove it back. The small croc's claws dug deep gouges as the beast skidded across the ground. The small croc slammed back-first into the base of Grant's tree.

A vibration worked its way up the trunk and gave Grant's quieting inner ear another round of unwanted stimulus. He moaned and pressed his face against the spiky bark. He got a good whiff of his vomit on the tree and wretched up a bit more.

On the ground, the large croc gave no quarter. With the youngster's underside exposed, the larger croc attacked, stomping one foot on the younger one's chest. It sent its long, black claws into the croc's flesh, then with one downward stroke shredded the skin. The wounded croc bellowed in pain. Blood and organs burst from the creature's gut and spilled out in a red, viscous rush all over the ground. The animal shuddered and went still.

The victorious monster let fly a roar that vibrated Grant's tree. The croc spun around and its great tail slapped the vanquished corpse, as if delivering one last measure of indignity. The croc huffed and shuffled back out of the clearing.

Grant was done. His limbs went slack and he slid down the palm tree like a fireman down a pole. The bark raked his skin but he was too nauseous, exhausted, and relieved to care. He hit the ground on his butt and felt the impact all the way up his spine. He released the tree and fell flat on his back.

"What do you know," he exhaled. "Still not dead."

The rest of the group climbed down from their trees. Wilson went over to the remains of Jorgenson's mutilated body. The rest came over to Grant.

Marie knelt by his side. He could barely see her through the haze of dirt and crocodile blood on his glasses.

"Are you okay?" she said.

"Nothing broken except maybe my coccyx," he said.

Kaelo stepped up to Grant's other side and the two of them helped him to his feet. Grant wobbled like a newborn colt. His leg muscles had already worked enough for the day, perhaps the week.

Marie let him go and stepped back, wrinkling her nose and turning away. Grant realized just how much of him was soiled with vomit.

"As soon as we find a body of water that isn't full of killer monsters," Grant said, "I'm going to scrub myself raw."

"The rest of us would appreciate that," Kaelo said.

The tail of the dead croc stretched out before Grant. "Marie, this ought to be enough crocodile for that Cajun recipe."

"Why didn't that thing eat us after killing the other croc?" McGinty said.

"It wasn't hungry," Grant said. "That fight was about turf and power, not food."

"Then we should get off its turf," Allen said.

The devastated looking captain rejoined the group. "Jorgenson. Soto. The whole crew. I didn't prepare them for this nightmare. We're a pleasure yacht, not some warship sent out to fight pirates and giant monsters."

Marie rested a hand on his shoulder. "No one could know this was going to happen."

Wilson hung his head. "What will I tell their families? Even I can't believe what's happening and I'm living through it."

Grant realized he had only one shoe on. He searched the sand churned up by the crocodile battle and saw the other one's sole half buried. He went over and pulled it out. A crocodile claw had slashed through the tongue and laces. The shoe reminded him of a baked potato, split open and ready for a helping of sour cream and bacon bits, which then reminded him how long it had been since he'd eaten anything. The shoe wasn't usable footwear.

Kaelo joined him as he stared at his flayed shoe.

"So here are my options," Grant said. "Going barefoot and subjecting both of my uncalloused feet to whatever is sticking out of the sand, or protect one foot with a shoe and hop around looking and feeling ridiculous."

"Another option," Kaelo said.

He plucked a fallen palm branch from the ground. With his teeth he nicked the tip of one blade and then split a thin strip along the length of the frond. It curled into a spiral.

"Twist strips of this together," he said. "Then sew your shoe back up. Palm is surprisingly strong."

Grant folded the strip over on itself and gave the strands a few twists. Then he pulled away the parted laces and replaced them with the palm strands. He put on the shoe, tightened up what he could, and wound the rest of the frond around the shoe and then his ankle. When he was done, the shoe stayed on his foot.

"I'll be damned. Looks weird, works great."

Kaelo turned to Allen, "There's more the island has to offer, and we'll need to take advantage of it to survive. We should gather up the coconuts and get away from this carcass. I need to find something to turn into weapons."

"Against a giant crocodile that bullets didn't bother?" McGinty said.

"You can stay completely defenseless if that makes you happy," Grant said. "I'll take a helping of whatever Kaelo's offering."

"So will I," Allen said to Kaelo. "We also need to be in a better position so those things can't ambush us again. The east side of the atoll is the narrowest, as much coral as island. There will be less jungle for them to hide in, and an easier place to catch the attention of my men when they come searching. We'll head in that direction."

Grant used the remains of the palm frond to scrape as much of himself clean as possible. The group lined up behind Allen as he began the trek for the atoll's far side. Out of respect for the olfactory senses of the others, Grant took up the position of last in line.

He hoped the giant croc wasn't in the mood to follow them.

CHAPTER FIFTEEN

The group made their way through the jungle. They passed a depression filled with welled-up saltwater. Grant saw the opportunity to get a little cleaner.

"Say, you folks mind if I--"

The group practically shouted a "yes" in a chorused response. Grant was a little embarrassed by the vehemence of their permission.

A quick scrub with palm leaves and the water seemed to make a difference. Grant rejoined the group.

"Fresh as a daisy," he said to Marie.

"Let's just say 'a little better'," she replied.

A bit further on, the canopy cleared away. They arrived to find that a stand of larger hardwood trees had been ripped from their roots and now their bleached bones lay on the sand in great piles.

"Knocked down by crocodiles?" Marie said.

"Knocked down by the wind," Kaelo said. "A typhoon perhaps, or a tornado spawned by one. One tree blew over and took others with it. All that torn up soil loosened more roots, rain washed away more earth, and you get a localized catastrophe."

"Which we can work to our advantage," McGinty said. "The trees almost make a circle. We can rearrange a few to complete it, make a safe place for a rest."

"Wouldn't that be outside the project scope?" Allen said with a smile.

"I'll make an exception. It wouldn't be enough to keep a crocodile out, but it would slow them down enough that we could get out the other side. And they couldn't sneak up on us."

"Good plan," Allen said. "Marie, can you keep an eye out for crocs or any other creatures this atoll may have?"

"Will do," she said.

Grant looked askance at the trees and broken branches. Some of them looked damn heavy.

"I had a childhood trauma with Lincoln Logs," he said. "I'm not sure I'm over it yet."

Allen slapped him on the back. "C'mon, Professor. Team effort."

McGinty led the four other men over to one of the larger trees. They surrounded it, bent down, and grabbed a limb. Sand and sun had worn the branch smooth and Grant had to grip it hard to keep it from slipping. On the count of three, they all lifted.

To Grant's amazement, they raised the log. Grant's arm muscles sizzled. He moaned, and then realized to his own embarrassment that no one else did. Allen led them on a shuffle over to one of the other trees. Grant stepped on his own foot with every other step. Sweat beaded where the sun burned along the back of his neck. His back started to feel like an overstretched rubber band.

"Hold up," McGinty said. He aligned his end better with the other downed tree. "Watch your feet and drop it."

All Grant heard were McGinty's last two words. They released the log. It landed on his right foot like a sledgehammer. He let out a scream. The others jumped back.

Grant dropped to one knee and shoveled away the sand under his right foot with his hands. His foot sank into the sand. The pressure on it relented, but the pain did not. He pulled his foot free and plopped down on his butt.

"What part of 'watch your feet' did you not understand?" Allen said.

"All of it, apparently." Grant took off his shoe. He flexed his toes. All of them moved without making a crunchy sound.

"Did you break it?" Wilson asked.

"Nope. But I'm sure it will bruise nicely."

"Then let's get another tree moved," McGinty said.

"I wouldn't want to miss the chance to get my left foot to match," Grant said.

A half hour later, they'd made a rough ring with the trees and interlocked some branches on top of them. Even if it provided just the illusion of security, that was still a plus. Allen picked his way through the barricade to scout ahead. McGinty busied himself with adding reinforcing branches to the makeshift defenses.

Wilson sat in a few slivers of shade beside one of the fallen trees. Grant dropped down beside him. The captain stared off at nothing with a pensive look on his face.

"This pleasure cruise has turned into a real bushel of crap, hasn't it?" Wilson said.

"If I didn't have lousy days," Grant said, "I'd have no days at all. Sorry about the crewmen who died."

"It's not something I've had to deal with before. It's not something I'd even considered I'd have to deal with. I mean, we're crewing a billionaire's yacht. It's not like we were manning an icebreaker or rounding Cape of Good Hope in winter. As maritime jobs go, *Endeavor* was the cushiest you could ask for. None of us expected pirates."

"They're not as entertaining as they are in the movies."

"And giant monster crocodiles? Nobody could even imagine that."

"Absolutely." Grant thought about the recent adventures he'd had forced upon him. "Only whack jobs would think giant monsters existed."

"And if I get out of this alive, Rothman will fire me, there will be an investigation about the sinking, and that's the end of my career. No one hires a captain that loses his ship and crew."

"We'll all testify it wasn't your fault," Grant said.

"I was the captain. That makes it my fault." Wilson leaned back against the tree trunk and closed his eyes.

Grant did not envy what lay ahead for the captain. He rose and slipped away to give the poor guy some space. At the other side of the ring, Kaelo sat on a log. He had his knife in one hand and a four-foot-long branch in the other. With precise, slow strokes, he stripped away the bark. Grant went over to see what he was working on.

"What are you making?" Grant asked.

"An 'akau tav, or a Tongan war club."

"To fight giant crocodiles?"

"You can use your fingernails if you prefer."

Grant looked down at his hands. "Tell me more about this club thing."

"These are the traditional weapons of the Tongan people. Today they're more ceremonial, more ornate. But two hundred years ago, they were the assault rifle of their day."

Kaelo flipped the stick around to the bulbous, uncut end. With several sharp, strong strokes, he chipped the end into a wide, pointed edge.

"Some are finished with a rounded heavy end for beating the enemy into submission, but that won't help us against these crocodiles. I'm using a different design, finishing the end into a blade."

"A blade sharp enough to do any damage?"

"Sharp enough to sever a man's head with one swing."

Grant ran his hand over his neck and winced. "That's pretty sharp."

"We used to hunt crocodiles with clubs like this. Drive the blade into the gaps between the thicker part of the crocodile's skin, or into the thinner skin of its belly."

"Make mine fifteen feet long," Grant said. "I don't see myself getting close enough to the underbelly of a giant crocodile to use one that short."

"How close you get is up to the crocodile, not you."

Grant had to admit that was probably true. He'd seen these things move, and no way in hell he was going to outsprint one. Kaelo went back to work. Grant went over to where Marie knelt beside two big coral clumps with the pile of coconuts.

"If you tell me you're preparing something to eat," Grant said, "I will bow down and worship you."

"Since I didn't build our little fort," Marie said, "I will contribute in a different way. First, hydration."

She placed a coconut on the coral and took a kitchen knife from her fanny pack.

"You brought a knife?" Grant said.

"A panic move to defend myself against pirates," she said. "Kind of a dumb idea, but it is about to come in handy."

Marie drove the knife into the coconut near one end. Then she turned it upright and sawed the top off like she was cracking open a soft-boiled egg. She handed the coconut to Grant.

"Drink up!"

Grant peered inside. A clear liquid filled the center of the coconut. He tipped up the coconut and let the water drizzle into his mouth. It was cold, sweet, and delicious.

"Wow." Grant handed the coconut back to Marie.

She smiled one of her dazzling smiles. "Better than what comes in a bottle, no? Now I will prepare the meat."

"This will be enough to keep us going?"

"Of course. Coconut is packed with nutrients. Lots of copper, selenium, iron, magnesium, and zinc."

"Am I eating coconut or strip mine tailings?"

Marie ignored his joke. "Most important, it has fat. We are going to need the calories."

She gave Grant's stomach a fleeting glance. He imagined her thinking "Even you" in French.

"We can survive on coconut?" he asked.

"For a while. But not forever, you know. It is over 60% fiber. That will have some intestinal side effects."

"Just what I need on an atoll without toilet paper."

Marie sliced a score line around the open coconut and then brought it down on a sharp point of the coral. The shell split open into two halves, exposing the bright-white meat inside. She scraped the knife blade across the meat and carved out several long white curls. Marie handed the coconut to Grant.

Grant plucked one of the curls and popped it in his mouth. He chewed and tasted real coconut, not the sweetened, artificial-flavor replacement all his junk food used.

"Oh my God," he said. "This is good."

"Fresh is always best. Too many people, they sacrifice flavor for convenience. I say, that is not a good trade. You should eat more raw coconut."

"Really?"

"Yes. It curbs hunger pangs. And the triglycerides in coconut burn body fat faster and suppress appetite."

Grant stopped chewing. She did get around to his weight after all. But at least she did it in a relatively kind way. He finished chewing the coconut and swallowed.

"I hope someone finds us soon," Marie said.

"So do I, if this is as good a laxative as you say."

CHAPTER SIXTEEN

Petra had spent over a month training to use the pseudo-submarine Green Warriors had provided. She'd been especially attentive to the GPS system. As far as she was concerned, the Pacific Ocean was damn big and Atoll X damn small and once she left the mother ship, she sure as hell didn't want to cruise past it.

She'd spent far less time getting to know the "team" she'd been assigned for this mission, three teenaged boys two decades younger than she was. Becker, Krüger, and Hoffman had all been recruited by Green Warriors out of the ranks of rabble-rousers who'd agitated at violent protests throughout Europe. Becker and Krüger had been runaways living on the streets. They would have joined any anarchist cause that provided food and shelter. But Hoffman had been another story. He was the first born of a father that managed a petrochemical plant in Germany. That one nurtured the spirit of an eco-stormtrooper and a deep hatred for authority. That one was going to go places in Green Warriors.

Now, after an admittedly miserable sea crossing, Petra had finally reached the destination. She stood in the cupola and gazed out at the swaying palms on Atoll X, just a few hundred yards away.

Her plan was already unraveling. There were supposed to be a couple of kids in a sailboat anchored here, ready to give her details about the atoll. There was no sign of the boat or of the kids. Maybe someone from Rothman's organization had caught them. More likely, they just decided to skip out and live the dream in the South Pacific sunshine.

Her supposed second source of intel on the atoll hadn't panned out any better. An insider in Rothman's organization on Nirvana Island was supposed to contact her by satellite phone. That hadn't happened. Petra could not call the contact and risk blowing the spy's cover. She couldn't call back to Green Warriors and risk betraying the entire mission. She'd been told to proceed without any intel if she couldn't get any. So that was what she had to do.

She started a slow cruise around the island to find an optimal place to go ashore. After a half hour watching unblemished beach roll by, she came across an arrow made of dead palm fronds lying on the sand. She stopped the boat.

Petra grabbed binoculars for a closer look. The beach below the arrow had been chewed up pretty badly, with long scrapes between the sea and the grass at the beach's edge, and big divots along the sides of those. She gave the edge of the vegetation a closer look. A gray raft sat partially concealed under some bushes. It looked like someone had come ashore and made a mess of things trying to get their raft off the beach.

She hadn't seen any other boats, so these visitors had to have paddled over from the Nirvana Island resort. If anyone knew what was going on here, these people would. Capturing them would be a hell of a shortcut to finding out what Rothman had up his sleeve.

"Everyone get ready," Petra called down into the boat. "We're heading ashore."

Petra revved the engine and aimed the submersible at the softest-looking part of the beach. Three teenagers sat in the rear of the boat's cargo area. Between the weight distribution and the churning props digging into the water, the bow rode so high that Petra lost sight of the shore ahead. She looked out the side windows to gauge when they'd hit land.

A wave rolled by and blocked her view. When it passed, they were practically on the beach.

"Hold on!" she shouted back to the cargo area.

A second later the boat hit land. The bow slammed into sand and travelled a few feet ashore before the boat lurched to a hard stop. Momentum threw Petra against the front windows. The engines kept screaming and Petra hit the switches to kill them. For the first time in forever, the boat was quiet.

Petra opened the hatch on the cupola and climbed out onto the deck. The fresh air and sunshine were a welcome change from the dim, stale miasma inside the boat. She leaned over the opening and called for everyone to get out. Petra walked to the stern and took a seat on the box that housed the emergency life raft, relieved that they hadn't needed to use it.

The three climbed out of the cupola one by one, wearing lightweight black cargo pants, black T-shirts, and carrying heavy weapons. Green Warriors had spent a small fortune on the boat, so they weren't about to skimp on firepower to get the mission done. Becker and Krüger carried American-made assault rifles. Hoffman's had a grenade launcher strapped underneath. The three took a long stretch in the wide-open space and squinted against the bright sun after so many days in the dark sub.

They were dressed like a team of mercenaries, but Petra knew better. These were three undisciplined teens with an hour of firearms training each, just a bunch of kids who thought one of their video games had come to life. They could probably get into trouble much easier than they could get out of it. If they were anywhere but a deserted island, Petra would be worried about what damage they'd do. But against some billionaire's lackeys, they'd be intimidating enough. She just needed to keep them from being too trigger happy.

The three of them reeked, but Petra doubted she smelled any better.

"Let's go," she said. "We have new friends to make."

The three jumped off the bow into the sand and walked up to where the raft sat in the trees. Petra checked the pistol and knife on her belt, then closed and locked the cupola in case some of their quarry happened to circle back before her team found them. She jumped off the bow and sank in the sand when she hit the ground.

A quick inspection of the boat revealed that running aground hadn't damaged the hull. The boat was far enough out of the water that it wasn't going to float away, but the propellers were submerged and could pull the boat back to sea in a flash. Perfect. She could even leave the anchor mounted on the bow.

She followed the three teens up to the raft. Whoever had come ashore hadn't left anything else behind.

"Make sure no one uses that raft again," she said.

Hoffman nodded and unsheathed a long knife. He pretended he was in a knife fight with the raft and jabbed the inflated compartments accompanied by bad imitations of Bruce Lee screams. The raft hissed and went flat.

Petra pointed to a spot where new footprints had beaten a path through the vegetation. "Follow their trail. Don't shoot anyone. We want them alive."

The teens grinned.

"I'm serious," Petra added.

Becker led the group inland.

A while later, the smell of something rank began to pollute the air. It was as if roadkill had been put in a microwave. Petra recoiled and wished she'd brought something to cover her face. She wondered if maybe there was some kind of swamp here.

Minutes later, the footprints of the group they were following led to a clearing with a few tall palms in it. The smell was noticeably stronger. Becker stopped suddenly and the others bunched up behind him. He pointed his rifle into the clearing.

"What the hell is that?" he said.

Near the middle of the clearing, a massive crocodile lay on its side. Something had ripped its belly open from its throat almost down to its tail. A soupy mound of guts lay spilled on the sand. Insects buzzed over the carcass.

Gross as this sight was, the size of the corpse was the shocker. In every dimension, this was the biggest crocodile Petra had ever heard of. It was easily twenty feet long and eight feet wide.

"Go check it out," Petra said.

Becker's earlier bravado had taken a vacation somewhere else. "Are you crazy? Look at that thing."

"It's dead, you baby. Go."

Becker shook his head and started a wary walk toward the croc. The others didn't move.

"What the hell are the rest of you waiting for?" Petra said. "Go."

The other two followed Becker. Their heads spun so quickly searching for danger she doubted they could actually see anything. Petra brought up the rear.

They made it to the carcass. The horrific smell seemed to seep into her skin. This creature hadn't been cut open; it had been savagely slashed. The skin around the wound had been sliced to ribbons.

"Look at the size of this thing, dude," Hoffman marveled. "Gotta be some like, mutant croc or something."

Krüger stepped up to the jaws and wrapped his hand around one of the croc's massive teeth. "I would totally hang this from my rearview."

Petra noticed a bloody lump nearby that looked like a human body. She walked over to see a mangled corpse missing some limbs. Its face was fixed in an open-mouthed scream.

"Oh, hell," she said. "This thing killed one of the people we're tracking."

The other three gathered around her.

"Whoa, bad day for that dude," Hoffman said.

"The rest of them got revenge and killed this thing," Krüger said.

"No way people slashed that crocodile up like that," Petra said.

A throaty bellow sounded from the edge of the clearing closest to the dead croc's head. Petra instinctively backed away from the sound's unseen source. The teens swung their weapons in that direction. With a roar, a massive crocodile came charging out of the trees.

CHAPTER SEVENTEEN

The three teens shrieked. Hoffman tried to run, slipped on a crocodile intestine, and landed flat on his back. The other two pointed their rifles in the direction of the charging crocodile and fired. Bullets whizzed by the croc's head and others sent up sprays of sand around its feet. It wasn't clear if any rounds hit the creature. If they did, the croc didn't care.

The panicked kids kept the triggers depressed until the magazines ran empty. Probably accustomed to the endless supply of bullets in video games, they kept pressing the triggers. Becker finally figured out he had to reload and dropped the magazine from the rifle.

Petra's drive for self-preservation kicked in. The crocodile headed for the kids at the carcass' head. She ran for the clearing's far edge. When she got there, she took cover behind a tree.

Hoffman recovered enough to make it to his knees. He brought his grenade launcher to his hip and fired. The round sailed ten feet over the croc's head and landed on the other side of the clearing. It exploded with a boom. Sand and chunks of grass rained down on the creature's back. The croc skidded to a halt to look back at the explosion.

That gave Becker the chance to ram a new magazine home. Krüger seemed to grasp his dilemma, and reloaded his rifle as well. The two brought their guns to their shoulders and fired again.

They aimed better and the croc was closer. This time more rounds hit the beast than missed. Bullets struck along the croc's neck and jawline. The croc turned back to face the boys. The gunfire wasn't even irritating it. It opened its mouth and hissed.

Hoffman pushed another grenade round into the chamber. He took a sloppy aim at the croc.

Then the beast charged. Hoffman fired and the round buried itself in the dirt near the croc's tail. It exploded and sent a cloud of sand everywhere.

The croc rammed Becker with its snout and drove him into the crocodile carcass. His ribcage shattered with a sickening crunch of bones. Becker's lifeless, broken body hung wedged in the reptile's carcass. The croc swept its head sideways and knocked Krüger sprawling through the dead croc's entrails and into the sand beyond.

Hoffman cracked open the grenade launcher and fumbled in his pocket for another round. The croc opened its jaws, turned its head sideways, and clamped them closed on Hoffman between his ankles and neck. His head popped off like the cork on a champagne bottle. The croc twisted its head away and revealed Hoffman's feet still planted in the sand. With a quick upward snap of its head, the croc swallowed Hoffman's body.

The croc stepped over and faced Krüger. The kid knelt, frozen by fear, covered in reptile blood and sprinkled with sand. He stared at the crocodile with wide, uncomprehending eyes, the look of someone completely in shock.

The croc advanced until its head was right over the kid. Then it slammed its jaw down on top of him. When it raised its head and walked away, it left a flattened Krüger crushed into the sand. Blood surrounded him like a hellish halo.

Petra was done with this. No one said anything about giant monster crocodiles when they told her about this place. She hoped the croc wouldn't mind if she left this party. She turned and bolted for the boat down at the beach.

She could barely think as she dashed back down the trail they'd made across the atoll. She stumbled and bumped into trees. All she could think about was being on that boat and being far from shore.

Behind her, the sounds of breaking branches and scraping palm leaves told her the croc hadn't given up the chase. She didn't dare risk turning around to check. Every second was going to count.

She broke out of the trees and saw the welcome sight of the boat on the beach. She ran across the hard-packed sand to the boat's hull. She pulled herself up onto the deck and went to the cupola.

A palm tree toppled forward onto the beach and the croc charged out of the trees, trampling the tree. It headed straight for the boat.

Petra fumbled with the cupola hatch and finally released it. She threw open the hatch and jumped into the pilot position.

The croc smashed into the bow. The ship lurched right and Petra's head bashed the right-hand window with a sharp crack. The anchor popped off the bow and plunged into the sand.

Petra started the engines and threw them into reverse. She pegged the throttle.

The boat didn't move. She looked out the cupola's rear window. With the boat cocked at an angle, the port side screw was half out of the water. It sent up a useless fan of seawater against the hull.

The croc bellowed in anger. The boat's hull vibrated.

Petra scrambled down into the cargo area. The humid air still stank of its unwashed human cargo. The whine of the engines rang in her ears.

She threw herself against the port side hull, trying to rock the boat back closer to level. Three times she battered the hull. On the fourth attempt, the boat shifted back to port. The splashing sound at the stern turned into a low roar as the prop began to churn deeper water. Petra scrambled back up into the cupola.

Sand scraped against the fiberglass hull as the boat slid down the beach. Petra watched as the boat left a sharp crease in the sand and an angry croc at the high tide line. The bow dipped into the water and then floated free. The boat accelerated.

Petra smiled. "Later, gator."

Anchor line played out from the bow in big loops. The anchor still lay on the beach. Well, she'd drag it all the way back to Tonga if she had to.

The last of the anchor line played out, then the rope snapped tight. The boat dragged the anchor a bit down the beach, until the flukes dug into the sand. The anchor line stretched and wrung a spritz of water out of its spiral with a sharp snap.

The boat stopped. Petra cursed. The anchor was designed to hold the boat in place against raging seas in a storm. No way the motors would ever pull it free.

Was she safe out here? she wondered. *Would the croc swim out to finish her off, or be happy that she'd retreated as far as she had?* Petra had no idea.

But the croc did. It waddled to the water's edge, opened its jaws, and clamped its teeth on the anchor rope. Then it began to back up.

Despite the engines roaring at full throttle, the boat moved back to shore.

Petra slammed a fist against the cupola glass. She sprang up and onto the deck. Pulling her knife from her belt, she went to the bow. The anchor line would be too tight to clear from the cleat, but nothing was too tight to cut.

The boat was sixty feet from shore and getting closer. The croc reeled it in with each effortless set of steps. If it got the boat far enough up on the beach, nothing short of a Biblical flood would get it back to sea again.

Petra made it to the bow and knelt where the anchor line wound around the bow cleat. The opposing forces pulled it harp-string tight. She put the blade to the rope and began to saw.

The knife made little progress against the heavy nylon braid. A few filaments frayed.

The bow struck the sand. Petra fell forward and caught herself with one hand. She sawed faster. Hope of parting the rope in time began to fade.

The boat edged a foot up the beach. The croc dug in its front legs and tugged at the line with a twist of its head.

That was the croc's mistake. Its teeth cut through the anchor line and the rope snapped in two with the sound of a rifle shot.

With the tension broken, the cut line whipped back at the boat. The end sailed over the deck and struck Petra in the face like a cat-o-nine-tails. It knocked her back against the cupola and opened a gash that stretched from her temple down to her jaw. Blood ran down onto her chest.

The boat shot into reverse. Petra grabbed the top of the cupola for support and stood up. Blood splashed into her eye and stung like hell. She climbed back into the pilot seat.

The croc rushed down to the water's edge. It watched the retreating boat and appeared to decide that it would consider this a victory. It turned around and headed back inland. Its tail made a broad sweep of the sand, obliterating the palm frond arrow, and sending up a cloud of dust.

Petra wiped the blood from her face and slipped the engines into neutral. The boat slowed to a stop.

With the hormone rush for survival subsiding, the gash on her face began to hurt. She didn't have a mirror to look at it, but by the feel of it, it needed stitches, and a lot of them. She went below and retrieved the first aid kit. A splash of alcohol to clean the wound felt like she'd lit her face on fire. Once that pain subsided, she checked the bandage situation. Nothing was big enough to cover the wound, so she settled for seven band-aids placed horizontally across the laceration to try and suture it closed. She had a bad feeling infection was still likely, and a horrific scar inevitable.

Petra assessed her situation. She had her pistol and a pile of ammo in the boat. She had a healthy amount of explosives stored in the bow, and she knew how to use them.

And of course, she still had the mission, to find out what the hell was going on here. She knew at least part of that was giant crocodiles. She had to come back to Green Warriors with something more than three dead teenagers to show for herself or her payment for services rendered might be something much more dire than she'd signed up for.

One of the boys had slashed the raft, so whoever was here before she arrived was trapped on the island. If she could at least get a hold of one of them, she could get the full story of Rothman's plans. That would be worth something.

Petra went back to the cupola and checked the beach. The croc was gone. She nudged the engines to slow ahead, and began a circumnavigation of the island as she made a plan in her head.

Step1: Find a new place to land.

Step Two: Find whoever was on this island.

Step Three: Make them talk, by doing whatever it took.

CHAPTER EIGHTEEN

A stomach full of coconut combined with a drop in his adrenaline level had sent Grant into a light doze inside the group's makeshift barricade. He drifted away to a world where he was still on Nirvana Island experiencing the warm sun and the sea breeze. Cheeseburgers sizzled on a nearby barbecue.

At the snap of one of the nearby branches, he opened his eyes and returned to his uncomfortable reality. Allen climbed back into their defensive ring. The group stood and met him in the middle. Marie brought him a half coconut filled with shaved coconut meat.

"It's on the house," she said.

Allen took a mouthful and chewed it, smiling. "That's hitting the spot."

"What did you find?" McGinty said.

"A lot of jungle to work through. But what I didn't find were giant croc tracks, so that's good news. We should keep heading east as soon as possible."

"These should help," Kaelo said.

He held three war clubs in his hand. The ends had been carved into a wide, curved blade several inches across. He handed one to McGinty and one to Wilson.

"Didn't have time to make a fourth one," Kaelo said to Grant.

"I'm willing to let the rest of you take first crack at killing giant crocodiles," Grant said. "No point in embarrassing you all again with my ninja-like reflexes."

"Let's go," Allen said.

They cleared away a gap in the makeshift fort and headed back out into the jungle. Grant and Marie were in the center of the group, with Captain Wilson bringing up the rear.

"So, you do not feel emasculated now," Marie said, "with the other men defending you?"

Grant knew she wasn't trying to be insulting, yet she still managed to do it quite well.

"Well, hey, thanks for asking! And no, I don't. There weren't enough weapons for everyone, that's all."

"But you were last on the list."

"A childhood of being picked last for teams gave me the edge there."

In this stretch of ground, the canopy opened up. Knee-high ferns and broad-leafed plants dotted the ground. Allen led them straight across the field.

"There's no way this is an atoll," Grant said. "Not with this kind of vegetation and soil."

"If we live through this, you can write a paper on it, Professor," Wilson said.

To the side of the group, the plants moved. Everyone froze. Allen leveled his pistol at the location.

An enormous salamander crawled out from under some palm fronds between Marie and McGinty.

"Oh!" Marie jumped back, startled.

The creature stopped a few feet away. Head to tail the amphibian was over a foot long with a thin body and its legs had a wide stance. Sand stuck to its webbed feet. Oversized eyes bulged out on either side of its shovel-shaped head. Its skin had a slick, dark green sheen, except for a ridge of red bumps that ran down its spine. Its mouth turned up at the ends in a pretty good facsimile of a smile.

The salamander cocked its head at Marie and blinked.

Marie smiled and relaxed. "Well, look at you, Cutie. At least there's one animal on this island that doesn't want to kill us."

Grant leaned around her to get a better view of the creature. "Kaelo, have you seen anything like this before?"

"No," Kaelo said. "This is something new."

"It has some anachronistic attributes," Grant said. "That very wide head, the jointing of the legs. Reminds me of *Metoposaurus algarvensis*, a Triassic giant salamander. The same way those crocs have lived here in a time bubble for millions of years, these things could have done the same."

"What do they eat?"

"Insects probably. Tropical islands have no lack of those."

Marie gave it a closer look. The salamander bobbed its head at her.

"It doesn't seem afraid of humans," she said.

"It's probably never seen one," Grant said.

"Well, we don't need it slinking around here," Wilson said. "Time for it to get human-shy."

Wilson leveled his war club at the creature and made a feint for the salamander. It backed away.

"Beat it!" Wilson shouted and then charged it again, swinging the war club in front of him.

This time the amphibian stood its ground. It opened its mouth wide to reveal a bright yellow pallet. Then an orange tongue shot out at Wilson. It unfurled almost two feet and slapped Wilson's hand.

Wilson screamed and dropped the war club. The salamander scampered away into the undergrowth. Leaves swayed along the path of its retreat.

The others rushed around Wilson. Smoke rose from a spot on the back of his hand. A circle of blackened skin grew from around that spot.

"It's burning," he moaned. "It's like being on fire from the inside."

"Some reptiles and amphibians have toxins in their saliva," Grant said. "Bright markings on them are a common warning. Looks like this one is one of them. Probably evolved to keep from being eaten by the crocs."

Wilson tore away the bottom of his shirt and rubbed it hard against his injured hand. The smoke kept rising. Wilson's moan grew more pitched.

Vegetation around them rustled. Feet scampered in the sand. Three salamanders stepped out from under the leaves.

Grant grabbed Wilson's war club from the ground. Kaelo and McGinty leveled theirs in the direction of the salamanders. Allen drew his pistol. The group retreated into a defensive circle around the whimpering Wilson and Marie who was trying to help him.

Grant gripped the war club tight, as if he could squeeze some courage out of it to bolster the small supply he had of his own. It didn't work.

"Okay," he said to himself. "Three on three. We can do this."

Leaves moved. Three more salamander heads popped up around them.

"Why did I have to say anything?" Grant said.

The salamanders dashed for the group. Two headed for Allen. He leveled his pistol and fired at the closest one. The creature's head exploded into a red mist and it dropped to the ground. Seeing its mate die, the second salamander sheared away. Allen fired again, but this second round missed. The salamander darted in and out of the leaves a few yards off. Allen tracked it with the pistol, trying to get a clean shot at it.

A salamander each charged Kaelo and McGinty. The one heading for Kaelo stopped short of him. Kaelo crouched and held his war club up over one shoulder. The creature opened its mouth and its poisonous tongue whipped out lightning fast. Kaelo swung the war club like a major leaguer aiming for the fences. The blade came around and severed the creature's tongue before the tip touched Kaelo. The appendage hit the sand and wriggled before going still. The salamander screamed as blood gushed from its mouth. It rushed back to the safety of the leaves.

McGinty didn't wait for an attack. He charged the salamander facing him, pointing the edge of the war club at the creature like he was a jousting knight. The salamander didn't flinch. Its mouth snapped open and its tongue whipped out and wrapped around the war club. It scampered sideways and threw McGinty off balance. He went to his knees. He and the salamander began a tug of war over the club.

The salamander facing Grant showed no fear. But Grant had enough for both of them. It ran for Grant. He shuffled backward. The salamander leapt for his throat.

One foot hit a lump of coral and Grant tumbled down onto his back. He caught his breath and clutched the war club to his chest. The airborne salamander flew over him.

The war club's blade was directly over Grant's face and by chance caught the salamander's belly as it passed by. The blade sliced through skin. Blood sprayed everywhere. The creature landed in the vegetation on the other side of him and did not move.

Grant wiped the blood from his glasses. He rolled on his side to see how the rest of the team fared.

McGinty and his salamander were still locked in combat. Kaelo charged over with his war club at the ready. But before he arrived, Allen fired at the creature. The round struck its shoulder and its tongue released the war club. McGinty's quick victory sent him back on his butt. Kaelo arrived and drove the blade of his club into the salamander's side. Blood squirted from the wound and the blade passed through the animal and pinned it to the ground. It flailed against the sand and then went still.

The three panting men looked all around the clearing, waiting for the next salamander to attack. None came. They exhaled a collective sigh and relaxed. Grant sat up and wiped his face with his gooey shirt, which proved only slightly less than a futile gesture. Allen looked at him with alarm.

"Are you hurt?" he said.

"No." Grant pointed a thumb at the salamander carcass near him. "This is all a parting gift from one of our contestants."

Grant realized he could not see Marie or Wilson. He stood up and spotted them prone among the leaves and ferns. Wilson was flat on his back, his face slack and battleship gray. Marie was on her hands and knees by his side. Allen went over to the two of them.

"Marie?" he said.

She looked up at him. "He died anyway. While the salamanders attacked, I watched the poison drain the life out of him, starting at his arm and then spreading everywhere. Could it work that fast?"

"There are some snake poisons that work almost immediately," Grant said. "And an animal that big would have a lot of venom."

McGinty held up his war club. The area where the salamander tongue had wrapped around it looked burned. "We don't need to mess with those things again."

"Maybe we won't have to," Allen said. "Those salamanders may steer clear now, knowing we can put up a fight. But we need to keep moving to the edge of the atoll. No one will find and rescue us where we are."

Grant was about to offer some condolence to Marie, and then realized he looked like the victim in a slasher movie.

"Just when I'd gotten clean," he muttered.

Kaelo went to Marie's side and helped her up. She brushed the sand off her pants, took a deep breath and appeared to steel herself for the trip to the beach. She did not look back at Wilson's corpse.

"We'd better get going," she said.

Grant thought that woman was one tough chef.

CHAPTER NINETEEN

After a while trekking through denser jungle, the group hiked up a slight hill and came upon an open, scrubby area. A break in the trees gave a view of the ocean on the atoll's south side.

"This might be a good spot to take a break," Allen said. "We'll see anything coming to hunt us, and we can also keep a lookout for anyone coming to rescue us."

They moved into the clearing. A rough, fifteen-foot-wide ring of broken coral heads sat in the center around a smooth patch of fine sand.

"Finally," Grant said, "a place where we can join in a meditation circle."

"What an odd thing to be here," Marie said.

She walked into the center of the ring. The rest of the group followed, except Allen, who stood outside the ring watching the sea.

Even through his palm leaf-sewn shoe, Grant thought the surface felt unnaturally hard. He knelt down, swept away the sugary sand, and exposed what looked like gray, rounded cobblestones, each a few feet long. He turned to Kaelo.

"Are you sure your people never lived here? Between hauling up the coral and polishing all these big stones, someone went to a lot of trouble to build this."

"The only people to visit here," Kaelo said, "did it hundreds of years ago before the ban, and this is clearly not hundreds of years old."

Marie swept clean some cobblestones, then lay down on her back and closed her eyes. "Mmm. This is nice and warm and relaxing."

"Allen, you sure your men will know to look for us here?" McGinty said.

"Process of elimination. If we were still alive anywhere, the only place would be Atoll X. They'll come looking for us."

"So, what do you think Mr. Rothman will say when you tell him pirates sank his big boat?" Grant said.

"I couldn't say," Allen said. "I've only spoken to the man a few times. Wilson said Rothman had never even been on board the boat, so he can't be very attached to it."

"Never been on board?"

"It sailed here from America to support the resort. The few times I've seen Rothman here, he's arrived in the helicopter."

"He's putting all this money into a project and he's that disconnected from it?"

"He's not disconnected," Allen said. "He's in contact with all of us multiple times a week."

"He sends me new menu items every week," Marie said without even opening her eyes. "Even though we won't be open for months."

"He's just not here physically," Allen said.

"I'd sure be more hands on with this kind of investment," Grant said.

"The ultra-rich view money differently," McGinty said. "Big as this project is, it's a rounding error to him. Like you buying a few T-shirts."

"I'm an underpaid college professor," Grant said. "Even T-shirts aren't rounding errors."

A click sounded from underground. Marie's body, still prone across the stone, went rigid. Her eyes popped open.

"What was that?" she said.

No one answered. Grant looked to Kaelo. The man shrugged.

Another click sounded, louder this time, like someone giving a bit of pottery a hard tap with a hammer.

Marie sat up. "Don't tell me none of you heard that?"

Grant thought the noise came from right around where McGinty's feet were. Grant knelt down by McGinty's shoes. McGinty moved his legs wide apart. Grant swept the sand away to expose the stones. He laid an ear against one.

Something clicked inside the rock. Then came several other, more muffled clicks from farther away. He sat up and placed a hand on the stone. A crack spread across the rock beneath his palm. Grant jerked his hand away.

"I have bad news," Grant said.

The stone exploded into a dozen pieces to reveal a hollow interior. These weren't rocks the group was resting on. They were eggs. Out of the one before Grant popped the slime-covered head of a baby crocodile. Its mouth gaped open and it hissed.

CHAPTER TWENTY

Grant's heart skipped a beat and he high-speed crab-walked back away from the crocodile. In several other spots around the group, eggs began to break. Everyone jumped to their feet. The crocodile crawled from the egg.

The creature was almost a yard long, three times the size of a normal hatchling, and at least five times as heavy. Its body armor scales had a yellower tinge than the adults. The new hatchling spun its head around and eyed Allen. Allen went for his pistol.

The hatchling launched itself from the nest and clamped its jaws around Allen's arm. The impact drove Allen to the ground and his pistol skittered away and was lost between the eggs.

Grant rose to his feet and searched for his war club. It lay a few yards away on the ground. As he moved for it, eggs near the war club cracked open and two hissing crocodile snouts probed the air. Grant backed away.

Across the nest, a dozen or more eggs all split open. Hissing hatchlings emerged, snapping their jaws and looking hungry.

Marie jumped past Kaelo and out of the nest. A crocodile leapt after her. Kaelo thrust his war club at the croc and the blade struck it in the side. The strike deflected the creature and it hit the ground sideways, skidding into a clump of bleached coral.

Another croc made a run at McGinty. He held his ground and pointed his war club at the creature. It opened its jaws and McGinty plunged the club's blade into the reptile's throat. Blood gushed from its mouth and the crocodile bellowed in pain. Its jaws snapped shut on the war club shaft and McGinty let it go. The crocodile whipped its head back and forth, and then collapsed.

Allen screamed as he beat at his crocodile attacker with his free hand. With a snap of its tail and a windmilling of its legs, the crocodile spun like a chicken on a spit. It tore Allen's arm right out of its socket. A torrent of blood splashed on the ground and Allen shrieked. The crocodile scampered away with his arm in its mouth. Allen clamped his hand to his destroyed shoulder. His eyes rolled up in his head and he dropped into the sand, dead.

More crocodiles crawled out of their broken eggs. McGinty found Grant's war club and snatched it from the ground. Two crocodiles crawled toward Kaelo. He swung his war club in a wide arc at the creatures. They jerked their heads out of the blade's path and kept advancing.

The two crocs that had emerged near Grant snapped and hissed at each other. Then, as if they realized they were on the same team, they both turned their heads to Grant. The crocs gave him the same look Grant gave a piece of pie a-la-mode. He turned and ran out of the nest. He made a beeline for Marie who already stood downhill at the jungle's edge.

McGinty and Kaelo also came to the conclusion that survival demanded retreat. They abandoned the nest and were a few steps behind Grant.

"Hurry!" Marie shouted.

Grant glanced over his shoulder to see a swarm of crocodiles emerging from the nest and surging in their direction. Grant turned back around and tried to block out everything but Marie's pleading face. He pushed himself to run faster, but the shifting sand under his feet and his flaccid muscles refused to cooperate. Kaelo and McGinty sprinted past him. Behind him, a crocodile roared.

Kaelo and McGinty made it to Marie. Kaelo grabbed Marie's hand and they continued into the jungle. McGinty paused and shouted over his shoulder for Grant to hurry.

The sarcastic response Grant had on the tip of his tongue died under the weight of his wheezing breath and pounding heart. He made it to the jungle's edge and McGinty took off in pursuit of Kaelo and Marie. Grant tried to keep up.

As he beat back branches and leaves in his headlong rush to anywhere without crocodiles, he harbored a faint hope that the hatchlings would tire of the pursuit. But he soon heard the crash of vegetation behind him.

These kids were not giving up on their first meal.

The central lagoon appeared up ahead. The ground dropped off steeply before it. Grant tripped and stumbled as he skidded downhill. The baby crocs fell behind, perhaps more cautious about the descent. Grant tumbled and rolled until he broke out of the jungle to a narrow, white crescent of beach. The other three stood panting at the lagoon water's edge. Grant rose to his feet and staggered up beside them. He bent over with his hands on his knees to catch his breath.

"Did they turn back?" Marie said.

Grant shook his head. "Still coming," he wheezed.

The first crocodile poked its head out of the jungle. It let out a rumbling bellow. Other crocodiles nosed their heads out of the vegetation. All locked their yellow, slit eyes on Grant's party. Kaelo went into a crouch and held his blade high, ready to go down swinging at whichever croc was dumb enough to be the first to attack.

Grant sucked in a deep breath and stood up. He backed up until the warm lagoon water lapped around his ankles. He couldn't outrun the crocs. He couldn't outswim them. The three of them couldn't out fight the whole swarm. This was it. He was going to die the kind of awful death Allen had just experienced.

The crocodiles charged.

Water splashed behind the group, followed by a muffled thump. A large, metal arrow sailed over Grant's head and buried its point in the sand between the advancing crocodiles and their prospective meal. A red light flickered near the arrow's point, and then the whole shaft buzzed.

A barely-audible hum tickled Grant's ears. But it didn't tickle the crocodiles. They skidded to a stop like they'd hit an invisible wall. Then they turned tail and retreated uphill back into the jungle.

"What just happened?" Kaelo said.

Water bubbled and churned behind them. Grant turned to the lagoon just as a small submarine's conning tower broke the surface. It rose until the steel deck of a thirty-foot-long submarine floated awash in the water. The top of the conning tower rose about five feet above the deck. A hatch atop the conning tower popped open and a short-haired young woman stuck her head out.

"That emitter's battery won't last forever," she said. "You'd best get on board if you want to stay alive."

Chapter Twenty-one

"Wait a minute," Kaelo said to the woman in the conning tower. "Who are you?"

"She's someone willing to put a layer of steel hull between us and killer crocodiles," Grant said. "I don't need to know any more than that."

"I'm Irina Mason," the woman said. "I work for Mr. Rothman, just like all of you do. Now please hurry. If the crocs return, I'm sealing the hatch no matter which side of it all of you are on."

McGinty and Marie didn't wait for Kaelo's approval. They waded into the water and then swam the few strokes needed to get to the sub's deck. Kaelo gave Irina another once over, then followed the two to the sub. Grant moved to do the same.

"Wait, you," Irina said to Grant, as she pointed at the metal shaft in the sand. "Bring the emitter with you."

Grant wasn't thrilled to be the last potential crocodile meal left defenseless on the beach. He hurried over to the emitter, grabbed the top of the shaft with both hands, and pulled. It grudgingly released its grip on the ground and came free. Grant stood there like an overweight version of the boy Arthur in The Sword and the Stone. The metal shaft vibrated in his hand. Whatever frequency this thing was emitting, it was outside human perception, but it must have been dead center of the annoying band for crocodile hearing. He headed to the sub.

Grant waded out until the water was up to his waist, then realized that he couldn't swim to the boat carrying the emitter. He waited for Kaelo to climb aboard, then shouted for him.

Kaelo turned around.

"Catch," Grant said.

He tossed the emitter sideways at Kaelo. The throw came up short, but Kaelo was able to lean out and catch it without falling in. Grant dogpaddled to the sub and climbed aboard. The red light on the emitter faded out, and it stopped vibrating.

On the shore, the crocs charged out of the jungle, no longer sonically repelled. They looked at the people standing on the submarine's deck and headed straight for them.

"Climb in so I can button this thing up," Irina said.

Irina disappeared down into the sub. McGinty hopped up atop the conning tower and followed her down. Marie went next. Kaelo passed the emitter through the hatch and then descended himself. Only Grant remained on the deck.

The sub began to back away from the shore. The motion put Grant off balance. He lurched and staggered over to the conning tower for support.

A squad of crocodiles hit the water with a splash. Vague, horrific memories of a video of African crocs taking down a hippo came to Grant's mind. He pulled himself up to the top of the conning tower.

Grant climbed into the open hatch and promptly got stuck. His stomach wedged itself into the narrowest space on the tower, the area under the hatch before the tower widened out.

"Hurry," Irina shouted at him from inside the sub.

He wished he could. But short of a strong dousing with cooking spray, he wasn't sure he was getting into the sub, or that he could get back out of the hatch for that matter.

He looked to the retreating shore and realized he wouldn't have to worry about either outcome. The crocs were almost at the sub. They'd eat him before he could free himself in either direction.

"Get down here!" Kaelo yelled.

Grant's face went red from humiliation. "I can't. I'm stuck."

Curses sounded from inside the sub. A set of hands grabbed each of Grant's ankles and pulled. Grant's hips nearly dislocated, but he didn't move.

The pursuing crocs' tails churned the water and the reptiles closed on the retreating sub.

"Again, on three," Kaelo said. 'One, two, three."

Grant sucked in his stomach so hard he felt his kidneys crush. Down below, it seemed like all four of the sub occupants hung on both his feet at once. He slipped down.

Something caught his belt. For a second, he stopped moving. But the force was more than the old leather could stand. His belt broke, and Grant plummeted down the conning tower. He landed on Kaelo.

Irina stepped over them and pulled the hatch closed. She spun a big wheel in the center to lock it just as several crocodiles clanged against the metal structure.

Kaelo pushed Grant off him. "Do you mind?"

"Sorry!" Grant grabbed the edge of a bulkhead rib and pulled himself up. His beltless pants headed for his knees. He grabbed a belt loop with one hand just before everyone got a full view of his underwear.

Irina went back to the controls. A set of rectangular windows in front of a small ship's wheel provided a view of the bottom of the lagoon. The water was so clear it was transparent. She manipulated some levers and with a rumble of expelled air, the sub sank to several feet below the surface. The pounding of the crocodiles against the hull stopped.

"That was close," Irina said.

Grant rose from the floor. He looked around the sub. The compartment they were in stretched back about fifteen feet. Plastic seats faced portholes along the sides that gave a good view of the lagoon.

"If you work for Mr. Rothman," McGinty said, "why don't I know about this submarine? I'm responsible for all the equipment."

"For all the equipment on Nirvana Island," Irina said. "On Atoll X you're, well, almost crocodile food, I guess. Info on the atoll is on a need-to-know-basis, and Mr. Rothman apparently didn't think you needed to know."

"How did *you* know we were here?" Marie said.

"I didn't. I was going to launch the emitter further inland, then drop cameras to remotely view the hatching of the crocodile eggs. I got to the lagoon edge and there you all were, surrounded by a ravenous nursery of crocs. Something triggered them to hatch early."

"We were all on top of the nest," Grant said. "We didn't know what it was."

"Obviously, or you wouldn't have decided to have a picnic there. And I know who these three people are. Who are you?"

"Professor Grant Coleman. I'm cataloging fossils on Nirvana Island."

"You aren't supposed to be here for weeks."

"You have no idea how much I wish I'd gotten that message in time to stay home."

Irina turned to Kaelo. "You know Atoll X is off limits. What are all of you doing here?"

"We were on the *Endeavor* when pirates attacked the boat. They drove us ashore here and the boat sank. We're the only survivors."

"You're lucky as hell," Irina said. "This atoll has plenty of creatures lined up to kill you."

"We noticed that," Grant said.

"How about you take us back to Nirvana Island?" McGinty said.

"No can do," Irina said. "The lagoon doesn't open to the ocean. It did a few million years ago, but coral growth and volcanic activity closed it off. Ocean water filters in with the tides, but the sub can't get out."

"Why does Rothman have a submarine in this lagoon anyway?" Kaelo said.

Irina returned to the controls. She spun the wheel and brought the engine speed up. The sub banked to the right.

"Like I said," she said, "everything about Atoll X is on a need-to-know basis. I'm not about to make the call on what you need to know. That's way above my pay grade. Have a seat and I'll take you to someone who can make that decision."

Kaelo and McGinty didn't look at all happy about being kept in the dark. Neither was Grant, but he realized he was going to have to let this situation play out however it was going to. At least they hadn't been killed by crocodiles. He followed Marie and McGinty to the seats along the hull. Kaelo looked like he was going to say something to Irina, but then thought better of it and took a seat on the opposite side.

At the surface, Grant could see several of the crocodiles that attacked the sub paddling around, as if waiting for the sub to surface to give them another go at it.

"Looks like we didn't shake that float of crocodiles," Grant said. "They're waiting for us up there."

"They won't be there long," Irina said. "Crocs learn quickly that they need to stick to the ocean. They don't belong in the lagoon."

"Poor hunting in the lagoon?" Grant said.

"For the crocs, yes."

Suddenly an enormous silver fish flashed by the window. It moved so fast Grant couldn't judge the length, but it was certainly larger than the sub. It had a dolphin-like shape, but with a much longer and much toothier snout. It raced straight for the surface and one of the crocodiles. It opened its mouth and snapped shut its jaws with the croc inside. It swallowed the creature whole.

"In the lagoon," Irina said, "there are more dangerous things than crocodiles."

CHAPTER-TWENTY-TWO

Grant stared out the window in shocked amazement. "Oh my God, that was an ichthyosaur!"

"I really couldn't say," Irina said.

"I'm a paleontologist. I don't need you to confirm that was an ichthyosaur."

"That fish looked like the fossils you were working on in the hotel," Marie said.

"Exactly, only much bigger." Grant turned to Irina. "You use this submarine to study them? That's why there are all these observation ports."

Irina nosed the submarine down and bumped up the engine rpms. "I really can't answer any questions. I may have told you more than I should have already."

"If we can't leave the lagoon," McGinty said, "why are we descending?"

"Because your answers are all down here."

The water darkened as the sub descended. Irina checked some instruments and throttled back the engines. She leveled the boat and then threw a switch by the wheel.

High intensity lights blazed to life on the bow. They lit up an underwater structure that resembled a sunken oil rig. Huge supports on all four corners stretched down into the darkness. Riveted metal plates covered a boxy structure atop the legs. A smaller, lighter colored section sat atop the first. Light shined from windows that dotted that section.

"An underwater city?" Marie said.

"Research station," Irina corrected.

She piloted the sub under the station between the support legs. With a blip of the throttle, she brought the boat to a stop, and then cleared some of the ballast tanks. The boat rose. Something clanked against the hull aft of the conning tower and two green lights on the instrument panel lit up.

"We're home," Irina said. "Follow me."

She led the group to the conning tower, stopped, and pulled Grant to the front of the line, right behind her.

"No offense, but I want some people behind you to push if you get stuck again."

He wanted to say that he wasn't offended, but that would have been a lie. However, she did make a good point. "I'll be right behind you."

Irina climbed up and opened the hatch. A blast of humid, salty air swept down into the submarine. She climbed out. Grant hitched up his sagging pants and followed her up. He got to the narrow point at the top, sucked in his stomach and pushed through. He emerged on the other side and wondered if his broken belt had been the cause of all his embarrassment boarding the sub. Even if it was, he couldn't very well crow to the group that he wasn't as overweight as they all had thought after all. He stepped off the conning tower and onto the deck with Irina.

The sub had risen into a submarine pen in the center of the structure. The pen was half again as long as the sub with a ceiling about nine feet high. White walls reflected bright overhead lights that lit the place up like daylight. The group left the sub and followed Irina along a platform which led to a metal watertight door. As Irina reached for the door it opened.

In stepped Parker Rothman. Grant recognized him from pictures in news articles. His brown hair swept down to past his collar in the back, a hairstyle from the 1980s that he steadfastly refused to update, though the gray that speckled it must have been a constant reminder that time had passed. Grant was struck by how much shorter the man was in real life than he seemed in pictures. Maybe if you are a billionaire, you can pay photographers to shoot you at an upward angle all the time. Rothman's brown eyes narrowed in anger as he saw that Irina was not alone.

"Kaelo, Marie, McGinty? What are you doing here? Kaelo, you of all people know this atoll is off limits."

"There was an accident," Kaelo said. "We were on the *Endeavor* when pirates attacked and ran us aground on the atoll."

"The crew is still on the boat?"

"No, it sank. Wilson and the crew didn't make it. Crocodile attacks."

Rothman's face fell. "Wilson was a good man."

"A salamander on the atoll killed Allen as well."

"Allen? What the hell was he doing here?"

"It's a long story."

Rothman turned to Grant. "And who are you?"

"Professor Grant Coleman. I'm here to catalogue the fossils on Nirvana Island."

"Coleman? You aren't supposed to be here for two more weeks."

"Yes, everyone seems to know that but me."

"I'm sorry I brought them to the seabase," Irina said. "But they were being swarmed by crocodile hatchlings and I couldn't just let them die out there."

"You did the right thing," Rothman sighed. "We'll deal with the security implications later. Everyone follow me."

Rothman led them out of the submarine pen and down a corridor. They entered a mid-sized room with a conference table surrounded by ten chairs. A large window in the far wall gave an underwater view of the lagoon. Light reflecting through the water rippled across the entire space. A digital display beside the window read *Depth: 20 feet.* Rothman led them to the table and had them all sit down.

"All of you have been told that Atoll X is off limits, a permanent wildlife sanctuary. Now you all know why."

"Because the wildlife is murderous?" Grant said.

"In part, but mostly because all of it is endemic only to the atoll, surviving here in isolation for millennia."

"You can scratch the isolation part," McGinty said. "One of the crocs swam over to Nirvana Island and killed two of my men."

"That's not good," Rothman said. "That means the giant croc population is more than the atoll can support and they are looking for more space. I may need to intervene and reduce the population."

"It was already reduced by one while I was treed by one of the monsters," Grant said.

"What is this place?" Marie asked.

"Seabase Rothman," Rothman said. "The first completely submersible research station."

"It looks a lot like an oil rig," McGinty said.

"That was the basis for the design. But a rig always floats. I wanted this one to also submerge, so it can stay hidden from any prying eyes."

"And be better able to study ichthyosaurs," Grant said.

Rothman looked surprised. "You saw one while you were on the submarine? What did you think?"

"I thought about how we should leave them alone," Grant said. "These creatures were never supposed to coexist with man."

"My plan exactly, Professor. They live in this lagoon, and I want them kept here, safe. The atoll's off-limits status will make that happen."

"Not if you are going to build a resort on Nirvana Island," Grant said. "If we ended up here, someone else will eventually."

"An abandoned sailboat washed up on shore a while ago and it made me worry about the same thing. My plan was to expand Allen's scope to include more robust security for Atoll X as soon as Nirvana was up and running." Rothman's lips tightened into a grimace. "But now that will fall to his replacement."

"In the replacement's job interview," Grant said, "I'd be upfront about the poison-spitting salamanders."

"And crocodile nests," Marie said.

"I'm guessing this isn't technically an atoll, is it?" Grant said

"No," Rothman said. "It's the remains of a great volcano, but coral transformed it into a hybrid of sorts. The central lagoon is as deep as some of the trenches in the Pacific Ocean, deeper than I can send my submarine. More permeable sections around the narrow eastern edge allow water and smaller fish to enter and that keeps enough nutrients in the system to support the ichthyosaurs. I'm sure it's a real shocker to see prehistoric creatures alive and well, Professor."

"Oddly, not as much as you'd think." Grant tightened his grip on his sagging shorts. "What has your research team discovered about them?"

"My 'team' currently consists of Irina at the moment running the seabase. Just like Nirvana Island, Seabase Rothman isn't fully finished and functional yet. I'm supervising the completion."

"And how did you get here without anyone on the island knowing?" Kaelo said.

"There's a helipad on top of the seabase. The seabase surfaces each night under cover of darkness to purge the oxygen scrubbers and desalinization tanks and perform a few other tasks. When it's on the surface, Ms. Carla flies me in from Tonga. All very secret."

"As secret as having all of this built without raising any suspicions," McGinty said.

"Money buys silence," Rothman said.

"And it will take a lot more of it to keep this science project running," McGinty said.

"That's Nirvana Island's purpose. To funnel profits into Atoll X."

Grant turned to Irina. "What have you discovered about the ichthyosaurs so far?"

"Not a whole lot," she said. "They can dive much deeper than the sub, how much deeper is a mystery. I've seen examples of all different ages. There is active propagation going on here."

"Hard to believe there is enough prey in here to support them."

"The reef outside is unbelievably healthy and sends in a lot of biomass. Ichthyosaurs will eat damn near anything containing protein. I've seen them swallow swarms of krill as well as crocodiles and anything else that swims."

"They are naturally aggressive?" Grant said.

"They make great whites in a feeding frenzy seem like nurse sharks. Any sort of movement triggers an attack response."

"I had a cat like that once," Marie said. "I was never so happy to have a pet run away from home in my life."

"The ichthyosaur we saw made short work of one of those crocodiles," Kaelo said.

"And we do not venture into the lagoon except in the submarine. Being in anything less protective would be suicidal."

"The important thing now," Rothman said, "is that all of you are safe. I'll get in touch with Carla and arrange for her to pick you up tonight. She can take a roundabout route and get you back to Nirvana Island as if you flew in from Tonga. No one can know that you were here, or anything about Atoll X."

"What will we tell everyone?" Marie said. "The boat is gone and people are dead. We need to say something."

"Could say pirates," McGinty said. "They took the ship and kidnapped us. We were rescued and sent to Tonga where Carla picked us up and flew us home."

"My experience has always been," Grant said, "the closer a lie is to the truth, the easier it is to maintain it."

"Until then," Rothman said, "we have plenty of space, so go crash in our bunk room until the helicopter arrives."

Grant's stomach rumbled, as if demanding its needs be met. "As long as we're guests, how about some grub? We've had nothing to eat but coconut for a while."

"Don't get your hopes too high there," Rothman said. "We're on MRE rations here with no cook."

"You have one now," Marie said.

"She does supernatural things with those awful meals," Kaelo said.

"Irina, take the men to the bunk room, then take Marie to the pantry and see if there's anything she can do to improve our food situation."

"Will do."

"And all of you understand the need for complete secrecy about everything you see here," Rothman said. "The last thing we need are a bunch of thrill-seekers deciding to sneak onto the atoll."

"Absolutely," Grant said. "You can count on our silence."

As Irina led the group out of his office, Grant's last words echoed in Rothman's mind.

You can count on our silence.

Rothman knew he could count on his employees for that. But with so much at stake here, he wasn't about to let his success rest on the moral integrity of Grant Coleman. The professor wasn't invested at all in the operation. He'd sell Rothman out for a quick payday. He'd agreed to come here for the same reason.

Rothman threw the switch to raise the antenna for his satellite phone. It was true that there was no communication with the world from the submerged seabase, but he wasn't foolish enough to not find a technological solution for that for himself. The button turned green, indicating it had broken the surface and locked onto a signal. He picked up the handset and dialed Nirvana Island. Hisoka Nishimura answered the phone.

"This is Rothman. I got a disturbing call from my insurer just now. Where is the *Endeavor*?"

"Um, well sir, I wasn't going to contact you about it until we completed our search, but the *Endeavor* is missing. It went out to calibrate a new sonar rig and never returned."

Rothman made a few noises that feigned shock. "I was hoping you'd tell me the boat was at anchor outside your window and the report I received about the boat capsizing was a big mistake."

"And it's worse," Hisoka said. "Kaelo, McGinty, Marie, Allen, and your new paleontologist were all onboard."

"My insurer got a call from a freighter captain who came across the *Endeavor*. He couldn't say what happened. He picked up some survivors on a lifeboat nearby, but the details were sketchy."

"Oh my!"

"This is a terrible loss," Rothman said. "Inform everyone on the island. For now, have the second in command in security and the one in construction take charge of their operations. I'll charter another boat to keep you supplied, and arrange for the survivors to get back to Nirvana Island. We'll get through this, I promise."

"Yes, sir."

Hisoka hung up. Rothman returned his handset to the cradle and smiled. He'd spun a credible story Hisoka would make no effort to disprove, if he could do so at all. Marie, McGinty, and Kaelo would all get healthy bonuses in return for signing non-disclosure agreements about what they experienced here. The secret of Atoll X would remain unexposed.

The only information leak he had to plug was the visiting professor. The risk of him talking about Atoll X was too great. In fact, he might even turn it into one of those silly giant monster books he'd written. No, Grant Coleman couldn't live to make the trip back to Nirvana Island. All Rothman needed to do was find a way to make that happen without having the rest of the group know he was a killer.

CHAPTER TWENTY-THREE

Marie stuck close to Irina after they dropped the men in the bunk room and headed through the seabase corridors. She stopped at a door in the corridor.

"The kitchen is in here." Irina opened the door to a well-appointed commercial kitchen, complete with new sets of pans and gleaming ovens and stoves.

"No one has used this place yet for much more than boiling water," Irina said. "I guess you'll have to break it in properly."

"I can do that."

"It does get hot in here," Irina said, "not just from the cooking. The gangway on the other side of the wall leads down to the reactor and all the rest of the things that make the seabase work. There's a pressure hatch between the two sections, but the insulation between the gangway and the galley doesn't quite cut it. Anyhow, all the food is in the pantry at the end of the kitchen. See what you can do."

"I will!"

As soon as Irina left the room, Marie dropped her practiced smile. Playing the part of the food-obsessed chef with the big smile was getting very old.

That had been who she was years ago. She'd worked her way up the ladder from two-star to three-star to four-star restaurants. Then one night changed her whole life.

Her fiancé had been driving to meet her at work. It was raining pretty hard, but he wouldn't let her call a ridesharing service, boasting he was the safest driver on the road. Halfway to the restaurant, a delivery truck crossed the median and struck him head-on. The coroner told Marie the only good news was that he died instantly.

The truck had been driverless, one of a dozen autonomous electric vehicles being tested. The driving rain fuzzed out the satellite navigation link and degraded the optical sensors that traced the edges of the road. The artificial intelligence running the show was supposed to pull the vehicle over in this kind of circumstance. A software glitch kept that from happening. Instead of pulling over to the right, the truck veered to the left, and killed her fiancé.

The truck was being tested by Transpo Innovations, a cutting-edge vehicle manufacturer. They offered Marie a settlement, as if any amount of money could erase the pain of losing the man she'd planned her future around. She went to fight it, to really make TI pay for their sin. But her lawyer explained that TI was untouchable. The state had granted TI blanket immunity to run the experimental vehicles on public roads because of the perceived benefit of having a future with driverless vehicles. And who had negotiated that unholy deal with the state? The CEO of TI, Parker Rothman.

When interviewed on television about the accident (Marie mentally corrected the reporter's question to "homicide"), Rothman expressed some limp condolences and then justified the testing in the name of progress. As if Marie should be happy her fiancé gave his life for such a worthy cause as the profiteering of TI.

Her attempts to make personal contact with Rothman through her lawyer were rebuffed. He apparently didn't care about what he did to her fiancé, and didn't care what the effect of that was on Marie. That just made her angrier, even more convinced she would need specific, personal revenge, something she could witness and savor.

That was when she saw the ad for a chef to start up Nirvana Island, with Rothman's stupid face right next to the picture of the resort. It was the opportunity of a lifetime. She could slip past the multi-layered security he had around him, and poison him with his own food. And she knew exactly how to do it to make it look accidental. She'd see how well he accepted that "accident" taking a life.

She had slipped through his background check because she'd adopted the name Marie LaRue for her professional work, a name that portrayed more sophistication than the Polish surname her family had. The background check never matched her to the insurance payout made to her legal name.

But that connection hadn't stayed secret to everyone. Before she left Paris she'd been contacted by Green Warriors. They had a better plan for her. They needed someone on the inside at Nirvana Island, someone who could get the details on what Rothman was doing on Atoll X. A wild-eyed true believer named Petra would arrive soon after with a team of hell-raisers. Marie would give her the lay of the land, and Petra's team would wipe whatever Rothman was up to off the face of the Earth and expose it to the world.

Marie didn't care one bit about the group's eco-agenda. She'd been hearing greenie weenies predicting global warming catastrophe for almost twenty years and none of it had come true. But she saw a practical advantage to joining their team. Working alone, she might kill Rothman, but working with them, she could do worse. He'd be destroyed financially, his reputation ruined. And depending on what he was up to, locked up behind bars. She agreed to help their cause.

Green Warriors' offer worked out in her favor in another way. Rothman never gave her the chance to poison him. His few arrivals were brief and unannounced, the communal meals served buffet-style with many other diners. She couldn't very well poison that food. Rothman might call killing innocent people collateral damage, but Marie didn't.

Until two days ago, she thought she'd be embarrassed to report that she didn't know any more about Atoll X than she did when she was in Paris. But thanks to the mistakes of Captain Wilson and a pirate attack, that was no longer true. She knew more about Atoll X than anyone would believe. She would have been happier if learning all that hadn't almost killed her, but it was all working out in the end.

According to the schedule, Petra should be offshore by now, waiting for intel from her. She unzipped her waterproof fanny pack and pulled out the satellite phone Green Warriors had given her to contact Petra. She'd been nervous someone would ask to see the special spices she'd supposedly had inside the pack, but no one had. She checked for a signal and saw none. What could she expect underwater? Rothman had said the seabase surfaced every night. She'd get a signal then.

What she'd tell Petra would astound her. And everything she'd learned about Atoll X had inspired her with a new plan. Rothman was so proud of his seabase. She would make it his tomb.

CHAPTER TWENTY-FOUR

Grant had felt much more human after a shower. He'd spun his clothes through a dryer and fashioned himself a makeshift belt out of zip ties. It wasn't fashionable, but it beat the hell out of holding his pants up with one hand. Now he needed to silence his rumbling stomach. Grant followed McGinty and Kaelo into the dining area and let out a sigh.

"Finally," he said, "civilization."

This was no utilitarian science station cafeteria. Dark hardwood tables hosted elegant, high-backed chairs. Modest chandeliers provided wonderful light that set the white tablecloths aglow. Paintings of tropical seascapes hung on three of the walls. The fourth wall had a digital depth gauge and a single, enormous picture window that provided a spectacular undersea view of the lagoon. Light penetrated the clear water and lit the collections of coral that had sprouted around the window. Brightly colored fish flitted back and forth along the polyps.

Rothman stood at the far end of the table. Irina leaned against the glass, looking out the window. She turned to face the group.

"Any food would taste better in this room," Grant said.

"It has such a wonderful view," Rothman said, "I hated to let it go to waste."

McGinty approached the glass and gave it a close inspection. "How thick is this glass?"

"It's actually acrylic," Irina said, "and it's about a foot thick."

McGinty rapped on the glass with his knuckles. "Seems like it's withstanding the water pressure at this depth."

"Thanks a lot," Grant said. "Just when I was getting excited about a decent meal, you have to make me start worrying that pressure will crack the window and we'll all drown mid-dinner."

Outside the window, the head of an ichthyosaur appeared at the left side. Grant got a much better look at it than he had from the submarine. Its snout was longer, and wider than a dolphin's. As it swam by, Grant could swear that its large, black eye stayed fixed on him. The body past the head got much bigger right away, with a dark upper half and a sparkly silver lower half. As the reptile was midway across the window, its body blocked the view of the rest of the lagoon. Then the ichthyosaur tapered to a shark-like tail that swept the sea in broad, powerful strokes.

"Or," Kaelo said with a mischievous smile, "maybe one of your ichthyosaurs will see us in here and decide we look like tasty snacks."

"You definitely don't have to worry about that," Irina said. "Electricity powers a polarizing filter that diffuses any outgoing light. Anything the ichthyosaurs see is at best an indistinct shape. Even if they did take a run at it, I doubt they could break it."

"So, you only *doubt* an ichthyosaur can break the glass?" Grant said. "That's not very reassuring."

"You did say those things were aggressive," Kaelo said. "Have they attacked the seabase?"

"No," Irina said. "The seabase isn't moving, so the ichthyosaurs don't see it as prey. Same thing with the submarine. If I crawl along, they ignore it. I'm in no mood to speed up just to test their tolerance levels."

"Ichthyosaurs don't have very large or developed brains," Grant said. "I would not credit them with a great deal of reasoning skills. I'm sure they would attack an indigestible metal submarine if they thought it was a fish."

"By the time it bit down and found out the thing wasn't a fish," Rothman said, "it might be too late for the sub. These ichthyosaurs have powerful jaws. We've seen one pulverize huge sea turtles that ventured into the lagoon. One bite and then it swallowed it whole."

"The skin on that ichthyosaur did not have scales," Grant said, "but I swear it still looked silver."

"The ichthyosaurs have skin cells similar to some octopi," Irina said. "Pigmentation can change to match the environment. Swimming by the seabase it looked dark on top and light on the bottom, perfect camouflage from above or below. Resting near the coral, it could display multiple hues. Up near the surface where you saw it from the submarine, it will be much lighter."

"It's theorized that ichthyosaurs are warm blooded."

"I'm not sure about that. But they are air breathers, though you'd be hard pressed to ever see one breathe. Like turtles, the ichthyosaur can stay submerged for hours, days if it is just lolling around down here. And when it surfaces, there's no whale-like spout. Even though we know there are ichthyosaurs in the lagoon, you might never know from the beach."

"Perhaps another reason Tongans were told to stay away from the atoll," Kaelo said. "Giant crocodiles along the beach, and anyone who made it to the lagoon might have been snatched by a mystery sea creature."

"It's definitely no place for a vacation," Grant said.

"And that's why there will be no vacationers here," Rothman said. "Not even outside scientists until we know more about the entire ecosystem."

The ichthyosaur came around for another pass at the seabase window. Or maybe it was a different ichthyosaur, Grant couldn't tell. But this one seemed to eye Grant with the same intensity. He hated to think the whole species might have it out for him.

"How many of those things are out there?" Kaelo said.

"We're not sure yet," Rothman said. "We can't even tell how deep this lagoon is. I'm afraid that if I install a sonar rig powerful enough to map the vast depths, it will have a negative effect on the sea life. But there have to be a lot of them if they have a sustainable breeding population."

"Eventually the population would outstrip the available resources that wash into the lagoon," Grant said.

"When that happens," Rothman said, "we've seen the ichthyosaurs eat their young."

"Wow," Grant said. "And I thought my parents were strict."

Marie entered through the kitchen door pushing a cart containing several serving bowls filled with steaming food. The chorus of scents tingled Grant's nose and his mouth watered. The cart stopped beside him and he recognized an Italian pasta dish, a Mexican dish over white rice, and something he couldn't identify but smelled fantastic.

"I don't know what this is," Rothman said, "but these aren't the MREs we've been eating."

"Yes, they are," Marie said. "Just properly cooked with spices and some other additions from the pantry stores."

Marie served up healthy portions onto plates and passed them out to the group. Grant sampled the Italian dish first. It tasted so good it made his body tingle. He made a satisfied moaning sound.

"It's good?" Marie asked.

"Good? Let me just say that as soon as you are willing to settle for someone well below any woman's standards, I'll have a marriage license waiting."

Everyone dug into the food and seemed as pleased with it as Grant was.

Outside the window, a swirling ball of what looked like mackerel formed. The bodies flashed silver like a living disco ball. An ichthyosaur appeared and dove through the school like a torpedo. The fish scattered. The predator disappeared into the darkness of the lagoon's depths. Bits of dead mackerel danced in the reptile's blood-tinged wake.

"If a breeding pair of those things ever gets into the open sea," Grant said, "it would be catastrophic. There would be no stopping them."

"Unless they learned to crawl across dry land," Rothman said, "there's no way they can get out of this lagoon."

"From the submarine," McGinty said, "this looked a lot like an oil rig."

"The upper section we are in is designed for habitation, but the lower section is a scaled down version of an oil rig. Anchor lines tie it to the walls of the lagoon a couple of hundred meters down. Winches and the ballast tanks control the depth of the seabase. The nuclear reactor and all the other mechanical equipment are built into the lower section."

Grant choked on a bit of pasta. "Nuclear reactor?"

"A small one. The design's been used on submarines since the Cold War. Cooling water is chilled and reused to protect the lagoon. It's all quite efficient."

"Why is it I'd feel more comfortable wearing a dosimeter right now?" Grant said.

"Relax, Professor. This section is separate, the engineering section is shielded a dozen ways, and it's absolutely festooned with radiation sensors. You have nothing to worry about."

"I'm sitting over a nuclear device in a lagoon filled with ichthyosaurs in the middle of an atoll infested with giant crocodiles and poisonous salamanders. What would I have to worry about?"

"I thought the water would make the seabase move, at least a little," McGinty said. "But I haven't felt a thing."

"No, the research section is connected to the rest of the seabase by a set of hydraulic cylinders," Rothman said. "Computer controls constantly adjust the hydraulics so that no matter how much the seabase rocks and sways in the water, we stay perfectly stable."

"Ingenious," McGinty said.

"And it allowed me to build the research section independently of the rig and attach it later. Saved a lot of construction time."

Grant still wasn't comfortable at all being submerged in what was basically a metal box. "Let's say, hypothetically, there's some catastrophe here. Can we abandon ship?"

"If we're on the surface," Rothman said, "there's an emergency skiff beside the helipad."

"Let's say, hypothetically, we're submerged and this tribute to marine engineering springs a giant leak?" Grant said.

"We can escape in the submarine in case there was some kind of calamity," Irina said, "but I can't imagine a situation where we'd have to use it."

"My imagination is a lot more active than yours."

McGinty turned to Irina. "I've built some amazing things over my career, but nothing like this. I'd love to see the control room if that's okay."

Irina looked to Rothman. Rothman nodded his approval. Irina smiled.

"I'll take you down for a look after dinner."

"Excellent," McGinty said.

"So," Kaelo said. "The big question is when are we all getting back to Nirvana Island?"

"I'll call for the helicopter tonight when we surface. Carla is on standby and can be out in the morning to pick you up. You can all rest in your quarters and I'll alert you when it's on the way to the atoll. You should all get a ride back and be on Nirvana Island for lunch."

"Fantastic," Grant said.

"You want to leave?" Irina said. "Don't you want to study these living dinosaurs?"

"The opportunity to study living ichthyosaurs is appealing," Grant said, "but doing it submerged in this underwater sarcophagus is a dealbreaker. I want to see the next sunset from the beach on Nirvana Island."

Grant also knew from previous experiences that contact between humans and previously-thought extinct animals never worked out in the human's favor. Rothman said they could rest after dinner, but the anticipation of putting a nice expanse of ocean between him and the murderous beasts on Atoll X wasn't going to let him fall asleep. Just once, he'd like to get off campus and not end up experiencing an inspiration for another of his giant monster novels.

CHAPTER TWENTY-FIVE

Marie cringed over her missed opportunity to kill Rothman.

Fantasies of attacking Rothman had played out in her head from the moment she saw him in the dining area: stabbed with a carving fork, chopped with a butcher's cleaver, scalded with a pot of boiling water. The options were many and she had the tools at her disposal to do it. The idea of sneaking up behind him, laying a boning knife against his throat, and slicing open an artery made her pulse race. As he died, she'd whisper in his ear "This is for my fiancé." The delicious options were nearly irresistible.

But resist she did. Too many people might try to stop her, or afterwards try to save his miserable life. Plus, the revenge she had planned for him would be so much sweeter.

Dinner concluded and everyone heaped another round of praise upon Marie's cooking. As she cleared the table onto a cart, everyone but Grant departed.

"In the interest of keeping on the good side of the chef," he said, "I will be happy to help with the dishes."

That was the last thing Marie needed. "Absolutely not. You do not set foot in my kitchen for any reason. And that includes when we get back to Nirvana Island."

Grant raised his hands in surrender. "Okay, I offered. My contribution will have to continue to be restricted to consumption."

He left Marie alone in the dining area. Marie had not refused his assistance because she wanted to do all the cleaning chores by herself. She needed to find out more about this seabase, and she didn't need him hanging around to keep her from doing that.

Marie rolled the cart full of dishes into the kitchen, and then went and checked the corridor. It was empty. She went to the hatch beside the galley and pulled it open. It opened to a gangway with an open circular hatch in the floor. A vertical ladder beckoned to her from within the hatch.

She listened, but didn't hear anything from below. Her fear was that Irina was down there, possibly still with McGinty. If she was, Marie would just blame natural curiosity and that she was poking around to see what was on the other side of the galley. No one was going to suspect the cute little chef, anyway.

She climbed down. The ladder deposited her in a large control room. A Rothman Corporation logo danced across the touchscreens at workstations around the room. Signs identified what each station managed: Environmental, Power, Ballast and Propulsion.

If she wanted to destroy this seabase, overloading the nuclear reactor seemed like a pretty good place to start. Surely there would be no need for passwords among such a trusted crew.

She went to the Power workstation and tapped the touchscreen. Reactor diagrams popped up, accompanied by tables of data on power output, a dozen different temperatures, and a bunch of other settings she did not comprehend. She realized she didn't even understand how a nuclear reactor worked, let alone how to make it not work.

She looked under the workstation and saw a binder thick as a loaf of bread. She slid it out. The cover declared it to be the reactor operation manual and references. That confirmed that she was never going to know enough about this reactor to bypass the likely hundreds of safeties and get it to go all Chernobyl. Plus, she wanted this to be a disaster she survived.

The station to her left was Ballast and Propulsion. She went to that touchscreen and tapped it to life. Similar style diagrams to the ones on the Power station popped up. However, she knew how ballast tanks worked. Compressed air blew into a water tank and expelled the water. That made the seabase lighter and cables on winches controlled its rise to the surface. Refill the water tanks, and the seabase descended. When it got to the correct depth, air compressors kicked in to stop the descent. Simple. These screens made complete sense to her.

Marie realized that she didn't have to work so hard to sink the seabase. The whole thing was primed to sink itself with just a little help.

She looked under this workstation. The manual for Ballast and Propulsion was the thickness of a Belgian waffle. She took the binder and headed back for the ladder.

The sound of water rushing through pipes came from beneath her feet. She turned around to see a series of messages flash across the touchscreen. Red colored valve icons turned green. The recorded levels in the ballast tanks dropped as the air pressure in the reserve tanks forced the water back into the lagoon. The four cable winch icons went to unlock and the depth gauge on the screen began to count downward.

The seabase was on its way up. She had tonight to figure out how to send this thing back down, but that trip would be all the way to the bottom of the lagoon. Her only regret would be not seeing the look on Rothman's face when he realized what was happening. She couldn't decide whether she wanted him to slowly suffocate in the cold dark of the dying seabase, or drown when the water pressure crushed the hull like an eggshell.

She'd have to give that one some serious thought. Either way, it would be much more rewarding than poisoning him.

CHAPTER TWENTY-SIX

Petra had made at least four circuits around the atoll. Honestly, she'd stopped counting. The whole place looked the same; white beaches, palm trees and scrub. There was one point where the land narrowed to a white, rocky coral outcrop for a bit, but then it was back to the same repetitive scenery.

What she hadn't seen were any signs of human beings. There were no docks, no buildings, not even any footprints in the sand. There definitely wasn't an oil rig drilling for fossil fuels anywhere. She'd dropped anchor off the beach where she'd found the raft, figuring that whoever had been in it would return to try and paddle their way back to Nirvana Island. No one showed up there either.

Her assignment had been to stop Rothman's plans on Atoll X. But without any information from Marie or the sailboat kids, she couldn't plan an attack. And despite her circular reconnaissance, she was no closer to finding anything out herself than when she'd arrived. Petra wasn't about to go ashore in some random location and wander around exploring. She'd already seen that a plan like that could get you eaten by giant crocodiles.

It was late at night and she needed to grab some sleep. The wound in her shoulder felt red-hot and she was certain that some horrific tropical infection had set in. She wished she could have anchored in the protected lagoon, but the satellite photos were accurate, there was no way in there.

Her satellite phone rang. Dread filled her gut. It was probably someone from Green Warriors checking on her progress. Petra checked the screen and her spirits soared. It was Marie. She picked up.

"Marie?"

"Petra? Where are you?"

"Off the coast of the atoll. And if there's an oil rig here, you're going to need to tell me where it is because I can't find it."

"There isn't one. Rothman has built a seabase in the middle of the lagoon."

"No one mentioned a seabase."

"Because it hides underwater during daylight."

This revelation complicated Petra's plan. "I don't know how I'm going to get the explosives off this boat to sink that thing."

"Don't try to come ashore. The atoll is full of giant monsters intent on killing you."

Petra was painfully aware of that, but she wasn't about to share her mission failure history with Marie right now. She just needed to salvage it by striking hard at Rothman.

"It's just as dangerous in the lagoon as on the atoll," Marie said. "It's sealed off from the ocean and full of enormous prehistoric half dolphin/half fish things. The scientist here thinks they are the most dangerous sea predators ever."

Everyone Petra brought with her to the island was dead. There was no oil rig to blow up, and she couldn't get the explosives anywhere near the seabase that was here instead. All the sacrifices she'd made over the past several months had been a waste of time. Working in that awful coal mine as a cog in the carbon-spewing machine had been for nothing.

Then an idea came to Petra.

"I have a better plan for using the explosives," she said. "We'll set the monsters in the lagoon free."

"Nice idea," Marie said. "But how can you blow up a whole atoll?"

"Not the whole thing, just one section. The eastern part of the ring is the narrowest, more coral than dirt along that side. I'll set the charges there. Make a decent gap, and the water rushing out of the lagoon will do the rest of the work."

"Can you get the charges planted tomorrow?"

Petra thought it through. "Absolutely. We can blow this and you can hitch a ride with me back to a rendezvous with the Green Warriors' mothership."

"I'll meet you at the beach before you set off the charges."

"What about the seabase?"

"I'll take care of that and make sure no one makes it off alive," Marie said. "Except me, of course."

CHAPTER TWENTY-SEVEN

As he'd feared, Grant couldn't sleep. He was too anxious about getting back to Nirvana Island and away from the lurking ichthyosaurs that seemed to be waiting to eat him. At home, if he couldn't sleep, he hit the refrigerator for a snack. He decided to try the same thing here.

He wandered down the corridor to the dining hall. He stepped in and the view out the window had completely changed. The seabase had surfaced to a clear, tropical night. Dark water stretched out and melded with the silhouette of the atoll beyond. The moon reflected off ripples in the water and what seemed like a billion stars speckled the heavens.

He was about to root around for leftovers in the adjoining kitchen when Rothman stepped into the room.

"There you are!" he said. "Just who I was looking for."

"What did I do wrong?" Grant said.

"Not a thing. There's a phenomenon in the lagoon I thought you'd like to see. Multi-colored bioluminescent krill rise to the surface. With your scientific background, I thought you'd get a kick out of it."

Grant looked out the window again. "I don't see anything like that."

"The angle's all wrong. You need to see it from the helipad. I'll show you the way."

The phenomena sounded interesting and Grant needed a diversion, so he figured why not. "Lead on."

Rothman smiled and led Grant out of the dining room and down the corridor to a staircase. The metal mesh steps went up to a pressure hatch in the ceiling. Rothman climbed up first and opened the heavy hatch. Warm tropical air flowed down the staircase, tinged with a hint of flowers and the scent of algae. Grant followed Rothman up and onto the top of the seabase.

Soft red spotlights built into the seabase deck gave the area a rosy glow, and Grant could make out a lot of details. The entire top of the seabase was a flat surface with a large blue H painted in the center. The seabase floated in the middle of the lagoon. The water was about ten feet below him.

"The red lighting here is near invisible to any satellite photography," Rothman said. "Watch your step. The algae is slick as hell."

Grant stepped on the helipad. The soles of his shoes skidded on the slimy surface. He gained a new appreciation for Carla, the helicopter pilot. She landed on the pad in the dark and didn't slide off to become an ichthyosaur play toy. Rothman stood beside a railing at the edge of the helipad.

"Over here," he said. "Perfect view."

The slippery algae had Grant waddling over like he was teetering on roller skates. His paunch did him no favors in the center of gravity department. He finally made it to the railing beside Rothman and gave it a death grip with both hands.

"Piece of cake." Grant looked out across the lagoon. The water was dark save for the reflected moonlight. "I don't see any bioluminescence."

"Look closer."

Rothman darted behind Grant and pushed. Grant's feet slid across the slick deck and out into space. He fell on his butt. He held the railing overhead in a death grip.

"What are you doing?" Grant shouted.

"Saving the secret of the atoll," Rothman said. "Loose lips sink seabases."

"I've kept bigger secrets than this. Trust me."

"I wish I could, but too much is at stake. Goodbye, Professor. On the bright side you'll get to be closer than anyone's ever been to an ichthyosaur. Literally a once in a lifetime opportunity."

Rothman placed a foot against Grant's back and shoved. Grant's butt slid off the helipad deck. As he fell, his back scraped the edge of the deck until it stopped just below his shoulder blades. The rudimentary muscles in his arms sang out against holding all his weight suspended at such a painful, backward angle. He kicked his feet and caught nothing but air.

"You don't need to do this!" Grant said.

"I wish that were true."

Rothman pried the fingers of Grant's right hand from the railing. It slipped off and Grant hung by one hand. His pounding heart seemed ready to burst. His remaining fingers slipped against the steel tube. Water splashed as something big swam by underneath him.

Rothman slammed a fist against Grant's left hand. Pain exploded in his fingers and they went limp. Grant fell toward the lagoon.

CHAPTER TWENTY-EIGHT

"Perfect!" Marie said to herself.

She closed the Ballast and Propulsion manual and sat up on the bed. By skimming the manual and focusing on the big red WARNING sections, she had made a plan. She didn't understand how to make the ballast system run in perfect balance, but she knew all the improper settings that would screw it up. All she had to do was follow all those anti-instructions.

Set system to MAINTENANCE MANUAL OVERRIDE.
Release the locks on the cable winches.
Manually open the ballast tank valves.
Set air compressors to VENT.

Once the ballast tanks filled with water, then the piping to the air compressors would flood, then the compressors themselves. The rig would sink with no way to bring it back up. The cables would unwind until the cables ran out. The force would either snap the cables or rip the winches from the lagoon walls. Either way, Seabase Rothman would end up on a long dark trip to the bottom of the lagoon. Wherever that was.

And while all the panicked people scurried around the seabase trying to find out what was happening, she would be up on the helipad taking the emergency skiff for a quick trip across the lagoon to meet Petra and her pseudo-submarine.

She left her quarters and headed for the hatch to the engineering section. She paused as she passed the kitchen. She worried that she might encounter someone before her plan had been executed. She had best write herself an insurance policy in case someone tried to stop her from getting off this sinking ship.

She entered the kitchen and went for the carving knives on the wall. She remembered her class in cooking school going over the optimal use for each type of knife. Murder hadn't been one of the tasks covered. The cleaver was tempting, for the deep wounds its heavy blade could inflict, as well as the psychological impact on whoever confronted her. Seriously, who doesn't cower before someone threatening them with a meat cleaver? But the big blade would be too unwieldy. She chose an eight-inch slicing knife with a pointed tip. She wrapped a cloth napkin around the blade for a makeshift sheath, and then tucked the knife inside her waistband at the small of her back.

Marie left the kitchen and went to the open hatch to the engineering section. She climbed down and to her relief, the room was empty.

Marie went straight to the ballast touchscreen and tapped it. It blinked to life. Her fingers danced over the controls as she performed all the functions she'd memorized: tanks open, compressors off and vented, winches unlocked.

Somewhere outside a blast of bubbles surged against the hull.

"Yes!" she said in victory.

"What are you doing down here?" McGinty said.

Marie spun around to see McGinty standing at the bottom of the ladder. "When I came out of the kitchen, I heard noises coming from down here. What is all this?"

"The seabase controls." McGinty stepped past Marie and nudged her aside. He studied the ballast screen. He blanched. "Oh my God. From how Irina explained these to me, this is catastrophic."

Marie knew he'd go get Irina immediately. Her plan was about to collapse.

Marie pulled the knife from the small of her back, cocked her arm, and then sent it plunging into McGinty's back.

McGinty screamed. Blood gushed from the wound and ran down onto Marie's hand. The warm, sticky sensation startled her. She pulled the knife free and stared at it.

McGinty turned around. Fury contorted his face. Both hands shot out and clamped around Marie's neck. He squeezed.

The pain brought Marie out of her daze. Without thinking, she drove the knife into McGinty's stomach, over and over again.

McGinty's grip loosened. He moaned and blood bubbled from his lips. His eyes rolled up into his head, and then he dropped to the deck. Blood poured from his wounds and puddled around Marie's feet.

Marie stared at McGinty's body as the man's skin turned gray. She realized she'd killed someone. She had planned on Rothman dying, and the rest of them going with him, she supposed, but at a distance, indirectly. This was so brutal, so real, so…messy.

The sensation that she needed to flee the scene of this crime overwhelmed her. If McGinty had come down here, so could someone else.

Marie wiped clean the knife on McGinty's pants leg and then returned it to the small of her back. She turned to scale the ladder and noticed a small chemical fire extinguisher mounted on the wall. She realized that if Irina or Rothman got down here too quickly, they might be able to reverse her sabotage. It was time to make sure that didn't happen.

She pulled the fire extinguisher from the wall, and then bashed it against the touchscreens, shattering one after the other. A few more random swings at the controls turned keyboards into piles of chipped plastic and indicator lights into crystal shards. No one was going to save this seabase from any of these controls.

She dropped the fire extinguisher. It hit the red puddle of blood and splattered her shoes. She dashed to the ladder and climbed up several rungs. A quick look back at the room revealed bloody footprints that made a tattletale trail to the ladder's base. The sight made her shiver. Marie kicked off her shoes and let them fall down to the deck.

There was no turning back now. In for a penny, in for a pound, as her fiancé used to say. And it was for her fiancé she was doing all of this.

She scaled the ladder, on her way to escape the sinking seabase.

CHAPTER TWENTY-NINE

As Grant fell toward the lagoon, he closed his eyes and offered up a prayer that he could peacefully drown before an ichthyosaur spotted him as an easy food source.

He landed on something much harder than water, much earlier than he expected. His skull bounced against something decidedly solid and he saw a flash of stars. He opened his eyes. He'd landed on a catwalk around the perimeter of this section of the seabase, about six feet below the helipad deck. An emergency evacuation skiff was mounted at the catwalk's far end.

"What do you know," he said to himself. "Still not dead."

Rothman looked over the side and spied Grant sprawled out on the catwalk.

"Holy Hell," he said. "Now I have to come down there and roll you into the lagoon."

Suddenly an explosion of bubbles churned the water beneath Grant. The seabase shuddered and Grant swore he felt it drop.

Rothman's face screwed up in concern. "Someone blew the ballast tanks."

Something boomed below Grant. The seabase lurched in his direction. He grabbed the edges of the catwalk with both hands to keep from sliding into the lagoon.

Rothman had nothing to hold on to. The lurch sent him rolling right over the railing. He dropped past Grant, screaming until he hit the water with a crash. For a moment there was quiet. Then came the sputtering, splashing sound of Rothman making his way back to the surface.

"Grant!" he cried. "Help me back up there. I'll make sure you get home, triple what I'm paying you."

With the canted angle of the seabase, Grant couldn't do anything but hold on to the catwalk to keep from following Rothman into the water. Not that he was sure he'd help the murderous bastard even if he could.

Water churned around Rothman. He cried out just as a great set of ichthyosaur jaws broke the surface, wide open, one on either side of him. They snapped shut and the man disappeared. Then the great reptile breached straight up out of the water, inches from the catwalk. The giant snout slid by Grant, then came the huge black eye that still sent a shiver up Grant's spine. The ichthyosaur reeked like a stagnant pond, all rotting algae and decaying fish. Then the creature fell away from the seabase and landed broadside in the water with a tremendous splash. A wall of seawater drenched Grant.

The seabase rocked back to level. Grant relaxed his grip.

"I'm no longer impressed by the dolphin show at Sea World," he said.

More bubbles rose from the water below him. The water was almost touching the catwalk of the submerging seabase. The ichthyosaur might still be hungry, or bragging to friends about the food being tossed off the helipad. Either way, Grant wasn't up for taking a swim.

He rose from the platform. His vertebrae creaked and a big, throbbing lump rose on the back of his head. He'd bet his next paycheck that the steel mesh of the platform had left a checkerboard bruise across his entire back. To his left, a narrow set of steps rose to the helipad. He wanted to sprint up them, but all he could manage was a slow, painful climb.

The sun began to crest the horizon. As far as Grant was concerned, a new day could not get here fast enough. This one had worn out its welcome.

He stepped onto the helipad just as someone emerged from the hatch on the deck. The sun's first rays lit up Marie's face. He smiled. She must have realized he was missing and come up to check on him. He'd sensed their personalities clicking back on the island. It looked like she had, too. A woman who could cook and a man who could eat would be the perfect couple.

"Marie!" He waved his hands over his head.

She turned and looked at him. Then she sprinted in his direction.

That brought a smile to his face. He'd seen that sparkle in her eye when she looked at him across the dinner table. He hobbled to greet her, arms extended.

They met on the helipad. Marie pushed him aside and kept running. At the helipad's edge, she leapt and landed on the catwalk. Grant went to the railing in confusion and peered over the side. Marie stood at the end, ripping away the protective plastic cover from the emergency skiff. Then she jumped inside and pounded a big red button by the steering wheel.

The skiff dropped away and slammed into the water. The engine roared to life and Marie aimed the boat for the atoll shore.

Grant's jaw dropped. He wondered what the hell had just happened here. Where was she going, and why by herself?

The water surged up over the catwalk. He didn't have a lot of time to ponder anything. This seabase was submerging and he didn't need to be on the outside when that happened. Marie certainly wasn't going to be circling back to pick him up.

He turned back toward the hatch. Another boom sounded from underwater and a shockwave rippled through the deck. The far end of the seabase dropped. Grant's feet slipped out from under him on the algae. He landed on his butt, and began to slide.

Waves licked the lowered end of the deck. It was as if the seabase itself was determined to feed him to an ichthyosaur.

The open hatch beckoned up ahead to his left. His only hope was to try to angle himself to hit that and make himself into a human hole-in-one. If he missed, he'd be experiencing more about ichthyosaurs than he really wanted to.

He spread his arms out to his sides and slapped the deck. Gooey algae accumulated on his hands and arms. Grant angled his arms to act like brakes and redirected his body to the left. He overcorrected and was headed back toward the water.

He pressed his right arm down. But the accrued algae made him too slick to have much impact. The opening was only yards away to his right. The open hatch looked like a big hand, waving goodbye. He pressed his right arm down harder and tried to roll a bit in that direction.

At the last moment, he skidded right. The open hatch was dead ahead. He lifted both arms and spread his feet apart. He hit the target dead on. His feet sailed over the opening and he planted the soles of his shoes against the open hatch. The impact rattled his knees. But he stopped with the savior hatch opening between his legs.

He sighed, thrilled to have one of these near-death experiences finally work out the way he'd planned.

Then the seabase rocked in the opposite direction.

The soles of his feet left the hatch and he began to slide back across the deck headfirst. His heart jumped into his throat. He envisioned himself sliding off the end of the deck, over the catwalk, and into the lagoon filled with merciless predators.

He bent his knees and jammed his lower legs into the open hatch. The sharp metal edge dug into his skin as he hooked the opening. The seabase continued its slow roll and blood began to rush to Grant's head. He couldn't do this for long. He had an awful realization.

His life depended on doing a sit-up.

Grant interlaced his algae-slicked fingers behind his head. He sucked in a deep breath and contracted his stomach. His shoulder blades barely left the deck. He exhaled and dropped back down. Grant inhaled and tried again. He raised himself a few inches, then his hands broke free and he banged back against the deck. His stomach muscles felt burned as a rack of smoked ribs.

The pressure from the steel against the back of his knees pressed like knives against his skin. A vision of his legs being cut off below the knees made an unwelcome arrival in his mind, followed by the even worse vision of the hatch slamming shut and crushing him.

He interlaced his fingers behind his head again, this time between locks of his hair for more grip. He took one more breath and this time exhaled with a scream as he made a final try to get vertical.

He rose up forty-five degrees, then ninety, then almost to the hatch opening. Grant released his fingers and grabbed for the opening's edge. He touched cold, wet steel and hung on tight. The last of his breath petered out between his lips.

The seabase rocked back to horizontal. Grant was about to cheer when a wave splashed against his back and sent water down the open hatch. He realized that the helipad was almost awash. If he didn't get inside, he'd be dead. If he didn't close the hatch behind him, they would all be.

He wiggled his butt across the deck and dropped down onto the steps. The slick soles of his shoes slipped out from under him and he landed face first. Another wave rolled across the deck and sent gallons of lagoon water crashing down on his neck and back. He wobbled to his feet, grabbed the hatch, and pulled it down after him. Grant gave the wheel in the center several turns until it clicked to a stop. He collapsed on the steps.

Overhead, water crashed against the deck. A single drip fell from the wheel and landed on his lips. He spit it away.

He smiled, but then it turned to a grimace. What had he just worked so hard to accomplish? Sealing himself inside a sinking seabase. The uncontrolled way it was going down gave him no confidence it would ever be coming back up.

CHAPTER THIRTY

Grant rose from the steps and wiped the lagoon water from his face and glasses. He felt as slimy as a slug and his body aches had body aches. He staggered down the corridor to the dining area. He stepped inside to see Kaelo there. Morning light shined through rising lagoon water that already covered the window.

Kaelo's eyebrows arched. "What happened to you?"

"A little exercise on the helipad. This is why I prefer a sedate lifestyle."

"What were you doing out there?"

"Rothman took me up. He was afraid I was going to spill the beans about Atoll X when I got home, so he tried to kill me."

"Rothman? Where is he now?"

"Ichthyosaur early breakfast," Grant said. "I got back into the seabase just before it went under."

"I can't find McGinty," Kaelo said.

Irina came running down the corridor. "The seabase is diving and it's not supposed to jerk back and forth while it's doing it. Stay here."

Irina went down the hallway and stepped into the access way for the engineering section. Grant and Kaelo ignored her orders and followed her. She climbed down the ladder and they waited at the top. Seconds later, her head popped back up.

"McGinty is dead down there. Someone killed him and then smashed all the interfaces and switches. I can't access the primary controls and the seabase is in an uncontrolled dive."

"To what depth?" Kaelo said.

"To the bottom of this bottomless lagoon, wherever that is. I can tell you that it's deeper than the seabase is rated to dive. Which means that long before we run out of oxygen, the water pressure will crush the whole thing like an empty tin can." She climbed up to the deck. "Where's Marie?"

"She just took the evacuation skiff to the atoll before we went under," Grant said. "Didn't even ask if I wanted a ride."

"I need to find Rothman," Irina said.

"That would get messy. He's inside an ichthyosaur."

"I don't have time for you to explain all this. This seabase is going to be our casket in a few minutes."

"Can't we escape in the submarine?" Kaelo said.

"Not with the seabase diving. I'd never get out from underneath it without being crushed."

"How about scuba tanks, diving suits?" Grant said.

"You know how to dive?" Kaelo said.

"No, and I'm claustrophobic and a poor swimmer, but it would still beat drowning in an imploding seabase."

"We don't have any of that," Irina said. "The lagoon isn't safe for diving."

"I'm willing to hop a ride on anything that will float to the surface," Grant said.

Irina thought a moment. "Maybe the research lab could, if we detach it from the rest of the seabase."

"How do we detach the lab?" Grant said.

"You won't like it."

Irina closed the watertight hatch and spun the wheel to lock it. Then she rushed down the corridor with Grant and Kaelo behind her. At the corner of the seabase, she pulled an access panel from the wall. Inside blinked a small control screen and a series of switches and dials.

"Please tell me you can control the seabase from here," Grant said.

"No, all the primary systems are accessed from the control room, but I can get to the secondary hydraulic dampeners here."

She tapped the screen and it blinked on. It displayed a drawing of what looked like a car's shock absorber.

"There are four of these at the corners of the station to keep it stable," she said. "The hydraulic fluid runs through a cooling loop to keep it from overheating. I'm going to shut off the cooling pumps and then run the dampeners in a maintenance test mode until the fluid boils."

"I have a feeling I don't want to know what happens next," Grant said.

"The boiling fluid will blow the seals out, then the water pressure will crush the dampeners. The lab will break free and it should rise to the surface."

"Should?"

"It's basically a sealed metal box full of air, unlike all the heavy equipment attached to the rig."

A deep moan reverberated across the roof of the corridor.

"That's the water pressure starting to buckle the seabase," Irina said. "We need to hurry. You two should sit down."

"This is going to be rough?" Kaelo said.

"You're going to know how popcorn feels," she said.

Grant and Kaelo dropped to the deck and pressed themselves against the bulkheads. Irina threw some switches and touched some buttons on the screen. Red warning messages flashed up and she dismissed them. She pressed one more button.

The dampener diagram on the screen turned yellow. Then the seabase began to shake like a heavy coffee drinker with the jitters. A low rumble filled the air. The seabase bounced up and down so hard that Grant's butt left the deck. His already throbbing head banged against the bulkhead. He groaned, but all the vibrations made it come out as an embarrassing, high-pitched trilling.

Irina had herself braced against the wall with both hands gripped to the access panel opening. The yellow hydraulic dampener diagram turned red. Another warning flashed on the screen. She dismissed it.

The bouncing worsened. The rumble became a roar. Then an extra rolling motion kicked in. Grant's teeth chattered together and he clenched his jaw to make them stop. His eyes started to water. Every bounce against the bulkhead added a new layer of pain from the checkerboard of bruises on his back.

From overhead came the wail of folding steel. A crease popped into the ceiling like it was part of a magician's trick. Grant's heart skipped a beat.

"The imbalanced dampeners are torquing the lab," Irina shouted over the noise.

"If that update's supposed to make me relax," Grant shouted with a bizarre vibrato in his voice, "it's a total failure."

From what seemed like right under their feet came a loud boom, followed in rapid succession by three others. The control screen in the access panel went dark. The shaking stopped.

Grant felt like his eyes were still bouncing. He closed them, took a deep breath, and opened them again. Irina turned around from the panel and smiled.

"It worked," she said. "The dampeners shattered."

She headed back to the dining hall. Kaelo jumped up and followed her.

Grant felt like he'd been run through a rock tumbler. He used the support of the bulkhead to get to his feet and then followed the other two to the dining hall. Inside, the sea still filled the window. The numbers on the depth display were static at 410 feet.

"We stopped sinking," she said, "and just above design depth."

Off to one side out the window, a set of heavy cables snaked by through the water.

"The rest of the rig is still going down," Kaelo said.

"It's tougher than this lab section," Irina said, "with a deeper crush depth. Since we sheared away the connecting passageway between the two sections, the rest of the rig may flood enough that it doesn't implode. The reactor is another story."

"Please tell me it's a tale with a happy ending," Grant said.

"It isn't. The pressure will eventually crush the containment around the reactor core."

"And it will make a bomb?" Kaelo said.

"More like a giant boil, but the released radiation won't be healthy at all, even inside here."

Grant checked the depth gauge. If indeed the watched pot never seemed to boil, he feared that the depth gauge would never seem to rise. But he still couldn't take his eyes off it.

It flicked over to 411 feet.

"You've got to be kidding me," he sighed.

Then it switched back to 410. Then 409, 408.

All three of them cheered.

"And up we go," Grant said.

He turned to the window to see the head of an ichthyosaur pressed against the acrylic, its big black eye staring down Grant. Grant caught his breath. The reptile sank out of view.

"For a minute," Grant said, "I was afraid that—"

Suddenly the tail of the ichthyosaur swept up and into the acrylic window. It hit with a thud that tilted the room and sent the three of them reeling into the bulkhead. The tail nearly covered the acrylic.

At the corner of the window, a single drop of lagoon water wept into the dining area.

CHAPTER THIRTY-ONE

The huge ichthyosaur tail slipped away across the window.

"I thought those things didn't attack the seabase," Kaelo said.

"They never have," Irina said.

"If they see motion and activity as prey," Grant said, "we've just provided them with a hell of a lot of both."

Outside the window, an ichthyosaur appeared at the lagoon's edge. It turned to face the lab and lowered its snout. Then with great sweeps of its tail, it charged straight for the window like a bull for a matador's cape.

"Oh, hell," Grant sighed.

The great reptile closed on the lab in an instant. Its massive head slammed into the acrylic. Pictures flew from the walls. The impact rolled the lab up on its side. Grant tumbled back into the bulkhead and landed on his butt. He looked up just in time to see the dining room table hurtling toward him.

He cried out and bent down to the deck. The table legs bracketed him and the table top missed his head by an inch. It hit the bulkhead with the sound of splintering wood.

The lab rolled back to level. Grant crawled out from under the table. All the chairs were also piled up against the bulkhead. Kaelo and Irina hadn't been hit and were rising to their feet.

"Is that thing going to give up?" Kaelo said.

"Maybe not," Irina said. "They tend to get single-minded about a hunt from what we've seen."

Grant looked over at the depth gauge. It had barely moved.

"That thing is going to crack us open before we get to the surface," Grant said. "Can't we make this thing go up faster?"

"Physics are physics," Irina said.

"This is where being able to throw things overboard would be a nice feature."

Irina thought a moment, then snapped her fingers. "The tanks! They're weighing us down."

"What tanks?"

"The seabase uses a desalinization machine to create fresh water. The extracted salt and concentrated brine are stored in four clear tanks outside the lab. They are detachable and the plan was to airlift the full tanks out of here and dump them in the ocean when they got full. We haven't done that yet and desalinization has been running non-stop for a while. The system is almost full. If I purge those tanks with the compressed air reserve, we'll weigh less, and rise faster."

"Let's do it," Kaelo said.

Irina led them on a dash down the corridor. Near the end, they came to a small room that faced the outside of the lab. Three circular hatches that looked like the inner doors to torpedo tubes faced them. Each was labeled as tanks 1, 2, or 3. Irina tapped a screen to the right and a camera view of the lab exterior came into focus. From the outside, the three desalination tanks looked like big, clear, plastic hot dogs sticking out of the hull. Something green and thick nearly filled each tank.

"This will use some of our air," Irina said. "But it should work."

"Hold on," Grant said. "You mean our air supply is limited in here?"

"The air scrubber was part of the engineering section."

"Great. I was worried there were only three ways to die in this box. A fourth method really takes the pressure off."

Irina ignored Grant's comment. "You two need to go to the controls next to each hatch. Find the button labeled manual purge."

Kaelo went to the hatch on the left. Grant moved to the middle hatch. The purge button was the last one on the control panel to the right of the hatch.

"Got it," they said almost in unison.

"Hit that button."

Grant pressed it. A sound like the flushing of an airliner toilet came from the other side of the hatch. On the video monitor, a thick, green cloud erupted from the bottoms of the three tanks. It drifted down and the three tanks looked clear.

"That should do it," Irina said. "Let's see if it worked."

They went back to the dining area and checked the depth gauge. It read 279 and was dropping fast. The water outside the window had brightened.

"Victory," Grant said. "One in a row."

"What will we do once we get to the surface?" Kaelo said. "Marie took the skiff and a swim for the beach would be suicide."

"And it's not like we can paddle this thing ashore," Grant added.

"The wind will push us there eventually. Plus, Rothman's satellite phone is around here somewhere. We'll call for Carla to come get us from Tonga."

"Or call Nirvana Island to send over a small boat," Kaelo said. "Rothman's dead, the seabase destroyed. The cat's going to be out of the bag about Atoll X one way or another."

"You're probably right about that," Irina said.

The dining area darkened. Grant turned to the window just in time to see an ichthyosaur blotting out the view of the lagoon. Before he could react, the creature crashed into the lab. A sound like the crack of a whip echoed in the room.

The lab rocked back from the impact. Everyone dropped to the deck. Then came a crash from the other side of the lab module. The room canted in the opposite direction. The three of them and a collection of broken furniture slid sideways and ended up against the picture window.

"That's more than one creature out there," Kaelo said.

"Apparently ichthyosaurs can hunt collectively," Grant said. "I'd like to live to do a paper on the discovery."

From deep below, an ichthyosaur came charging at the lab window. It struck and metal crunched. The impact tossed Grant onto his stomach. The lab went back to level. Something cracked behind him and a jet of saltwater soaked the back of his shirt.

He rolled over to see a split in the seam between the window and the bulkhead. The spray hit him in the chest and clouded his glasses. He scooted out of its way.

"Oh, no," Irina said.

"I thought you said the acrylic was unbreakable," Grant said.

"It didn't break, the hull broke."

"I'll take care of the smart-ass comments here," Grant said.

The split widened. The spray of water grew to a heavy stream. It drenched the far wall and sent water running into the corridor.

"Get out now!" Irina said.

The three scrambled for the doorway. The curtain of blasting water separated Grant from the exit. Grant tried to blitz his way through the water stream. It caught him on the right side and the high-pressure spray felt like a band of needles against his skin. The pressure knocked him off-balance, but he staggered out of it and through the doorway where Kaelo and Irina stood.

"We're screwed," Irina said. "We can't plug that crack. This room cannot be sealed off from the corridor. The dining area and the main corridor and every other open space is going to fill with water. Once that happens, we're going down."

CHAPTER THIRTY-TWO

The last thing Grant wanted to do was drown in this sinking lab module, especially if there was a chance his last few moments of drowning would include being munched by one of the ichthyosaurs. He checked the depth gauge. Three hundred feet and steady. Even a suicide swim for the surface was impossible.

"I can't believe that you didn't include escape pods on this thing," Grant said.

"It's not a sci-fi spaceship," Irina said. "The failsafe to surface the seabase was built into—"

"I know," Grant cut her off, "the engineering module."

Water from the leak in the dining area now filled the corridor two inches deep. The sound of the rushing water intensified.

"But maybe we can make an escape pod," she said.

"How?" Kaelo said.

"We just emptied three of them,"

Grant didn't like the sound of that at all. "No way in hell."

"Come on," Irina said.

She led them on a sloshing run back to the desalinization tanks. They stopped in front of the hatches.

"These are big empty tubes now," she said. "They're designed to be reusable, cleaned after they are emptied and sent back to the seabase. They're big enough to crawl around in. There's an emergency handle on the inside to pop one end off if a cleaner got caught inside."

Grant imagined being sealed inside a tube three hundred feet from the surface. Getting eaten by an ichthyosaur was looking pretty good.

"I hit the release button," Irina said, "and it starts a ten second countdown to seal the tank and unlock the clamps. Get in and the tank will seal behind you. When it releases, buoyancy will take it straight for the surface."

Grant mentally compared his rotund physique to Irina's svelte figure. He wondered if she figured in that the two of them needed radically different levels of buoyancy.

"Once it surfaces," she said, "pull the handle and pop the end. Swim for it and hope the predators are all busy with the seabase."

"This plan sounds crazy," Grant said.

"It sounds better than drowning here," Kaelo said.

"You don't have to go," Irina said to Grant.

Sloshing water slapped at Grant's calves. He gave the tank hatch wheel a spin and then opened the hatch. The stink of salt and minerals blasted him in the face. "Oh my God, that reeks."

"You can breathe the air in that," Kaelo said, "or swallow the water in here."

"Why is my life always reduced to making the least life-threatening choice?" Grant said.

"I'm hitting the switch now," Irina said.

She and Kaelo opened their hatches, then she pressed the main release switch. A timer started a countdown.

"I'm never going to a public aquarium again," Grant said.

He climbed through the hatch. The light filtering through the pristine lagoon water lit the inside through the clear tube. The tank was about ten feet long and wide enough that he could crawl around inside on his knees. But there was no crawling to do. The inside was thick with slime and he scrambled to stay upright. The briny smell became chokingly overpowerful. Grant groaned and sealed the hatch door behind him.

What if this thing sinks? he thought. *What if it cracks? What if I suffocate? What if I drown when I open it?*

He couldn't help but see this tube as his coffin.

Grant wiped away a section of the tank to get a clearer view of the lagoon. An ichthyosaur zoomed by the side of the lab.

A clamshell-type door closed and sealed the tank from the hatch to the lab module. He searched for the release handle Irina had mentioned, mostly so he wouldn't hit it by accident. He spotted a red T-shaped handle in the center of the tube over his head.

Outside the tube, the retaining clamps thunked. An explosion of bubbles rippled along the hull's side and the cylinder broke free. It rotated 90 degrees so one end pointed to the surface. Grant slid to the bottom. He wiped away another section of the tank facing the lab and saw that it was already a dozen yards beneath the tank.

He pounded a fist against the tank in excitement. He realized how dumb that was and cringed. He wiped away more of the tube and saw that the other two tanks were also heading for the surface. Grant's tube passed through and scattered a school of small, silver fish and he realized what a good clip the tanks were moving at. With nothing to breathe but the oxygen in the tank, the sooner he surfaced the better.

Down below, two ichthyosaurs circled the doomed lab. One of them rolled on its side and Grant got a look at its big, black, creepy eye. Once again, he was certain that the reptile recognized him. He chided himself for his paranoia.

Then the creature turned and pursued the rising tanks.

Grant's heart skipped a beat. The sound and fury of the bubbles must have alerted the reptiles, and the motion of the fleeing tanks had to make them irresistible targets. The tanks probably looked a lot more digestible than the huge lab module.

The ichthyosaur aimed for Kaelo's tank off to Grant's right. Grant held his breath and hoped the ichthyosaur would miss.

It didn't. The creature opened its jaws and caught the tank between them. Inside, Kaelo's silhouette flailed against the sides of the tube. The ichthyosaur dove down. Its jaws crushed the tube with an explosion of bubbles. Grant's stomach sank.

The reptile continued its dive, then made a wide loop back up to the surface. It leveled out and headed straight for Grant.

Grant's pulse raced. "Time to make fat work in my favor, for once."

He threw his weight back and forth in the tank, trying to change its trajectory and throw off the ichthyosaur's attack. But the tank kept moving straight up, and the reptile stayed fixed on its intercept course. At feet away, it spread open its jaws to reveal two sets of enormous, sharp teeth.

The ichthyosaur chomped on his tank. The impact threw Grant against the side closest to the creature. Grant got an even closer view of the teeth that were about to devour him. A cracking sound reverberated inside the tube. Grant braced his arms against the sides and prepared to die.

Then the tube shook violently back and forth. The reptile released the tank, and it stopped moving sideways and began to ascend again.

The other ichthyosaur had joined the hunt, but in competition, not cooperation. The two reptiles swirled beneath Grant in a battle of slapping fins and butting heads. The fighting beasts descended into darker water. Grant's tank bobbed to the surface.

The humid and stale air inside the tube felt like the approach of death. Beads of sweat formed across Grant's forehead. He chided himself for hyperventilating so much. He'd remember that next time he was trapped in a plastic sausage being attacked by extinct giant monsters. Unfortunately, the way his life went, there was a possibility that might actually happen.

The base of the tank thudded against something. The idea of another ichthyosaur attack sent a fresh wave of panic through him. He wiped some of the tank clean to reveal that the tank had struck the lagoon floor, not a predator. Another glance around the lagoon confirmed that the most threatening creature in the vicinity was a clownfish. The tip of the tube broke the surface and blessedly blue sky shined down on Grant's face. He pulled the release handle.

The top of the tube popped partially open, but that top was below the water level. Seawater rushed in the open seam, began to fill the tank, and it sank out from beneath Grant. He kicked his way up through the rising water and pushed open the end. The tank descended and left him treading water a few yards from the shore. He executed a sloppy crawl stroke until his feet could touch the ground. Then he dragged himself up the white sand and collapsed on his butt. He raised his face to the first bit of glorious warm sunlight he'd seen in what seemed like forever.

"Grant?" Irina shouted from down the beach.

She stood about fifty yards away. Grant raised one hand and gave her a weary wave. He considered lying in the sun here until he dried out, and then remembered the atoll had a healthy population of murderous salamanders and killer giant crocodiles. He rose to his feet and slogged over to Irina.

She was as soaked as Grant was, and a wet T-shirt contest was a far more positive look on her than on a pudgy paleontologist. He pulled his shirt away from his belly and tried to slap a little of the water out of it.

He got closer to her and was alarmed to see bright red blood on the side of her head.

"You made it," she said. "Kaelo?"

"The ichthyosaur got him."

Irina's face fell. "He seemed like a good guy."

"He was." He gave her head a closer inspection. "What happened to you?"

"My tube got a slap from the ichthyosaur's tail that sent it tumbling end over end. I bounced around in there like a ping pong ball in one of those lotto draws." She wobbled back and forth. "I think I hit my head."

The fact that she wasn't sure sounded an alarm for Grant. He looked into her eyes. Her pupils were two completely different sizes.

"You have a concussion," Grant said. "You need to stay as still as possible."

"This atoll is no place to sit still if you want to stay alive."

Her first steps were sideways. Grant got beside her and offered a shoulder for support. She clamped a hand on him. They shuffled east along the beach, heading for the narrowest part of the ring. The jungle petered out there to a rocky swell of white sand.

"You'll be a surprise to everyone on Nirvana Island," Grant said, "No one there knows who you are or that you work for Rothman."

"Yes." Her S was very slurred. "I'll be quite a surprise."

Grant wondered how they were going to explain all this. It wasn't like anyone was going to let the death of a prominent billionaire become an episode of *Unsolved Mysteries*.

In a few minutes, they crested the rise that made up the eastern ring of the atoll. The Pacific Ocean stretched out forever on the other side, all deep blues and bright whitecaps.

"Isn't that the skiff down there?" Irina said.

Grant checked the edge of the lagoon below them. Sure enough, there was the little powerboat run ashore on the sand. "Sure looks like it."

On the rise southeast of the boat, a petite silhouette stood highlighted against the sand. That had to be Marie. But before he could point her out, he noticed something else on the Pacific Ocean side. A long dark shape like a wide cigar floated offshore. A low pilothouse protruded from the top of the hull.

"Is that part of Rothman's personal fleet?" Grant said.

"That's no boat I recognize," Irina said.

Grant's thought went to the pirates that had chased them ashore. Perhaps this odd boat was part of their flotilla. But Marie was staring right at the boat. She'd be the last person to stand around awaiting capture by pirates.

"Whatever's going on here," Grant said, "it's not going to be part of our rescue."

CHAPTER THIRTY-THREE

Petra was damn proud of the plan she'd improvised.

She had to admit that she had trouble believing that there were some kind of extinct sea monsters in the lagoon, but that's what Marie said. Given that Petra had escaped an attack by giant crocodiles, her believability threshold for giant monsters had dropped pretty low.

When she had gone to inspect the demolition charges, she'd found out one problem right off the bat. She couldn't get to most of them.

The explosives were stored in the smuggling compartment in the bow, behind a steel door, practically the only metal on the boat. It seemed that the drug kingpins wanted a spot secure from any untrustworthy employees. The crocodile attack had buckled the front of the ship. The hull had been squeezed and the steel wall between the crew area and the bow storage had buckled around the door. It wasn't going to open again without a cutting torch.

She'd searched the boat for something to pry open the door. Instead, she found one set of explosive charges. Apparently the three idiots she'd brought with her had been playing around with it. She'd joked to herself that she could blow open the door, as if that wouldn't set off the rest of the cache.

And then came Petra's eureka moment. She would set them all off with that one charge. Since she couldn't get them out of the boat and onto the beach, she'd just get the whole boat onto the beach. The emergency raft strapped to the deck could fit four. It would seem spacious with her and Marie in it. The two of them would paddle it from the atoll, and instead of the Green Warriors mothership meeting the semi-submersible, it would meet the two of them in the raft. Why, the plan was damned amazing.

Then after she lodged the single charge against the bulkhead to the bow, she found out she had a second, larger problem.

Petra had watched mine workers using professional grade explosives. The whole detonator contraption Green Warriors had packed in the boat looked homemade, with sloppy soldering and a plastic box that looked like it had been recycled from some other purpose. There were several buttons on the outside, but none were labeled. A four-digit readout was mounted next to where two wires ran out of the box. She assumed those wires attached to the red and black terminals on the explosives pack. But the wires were green and yellow. So, did it matter which went where? That gave her only even odds at getting the thing to detonate.

Without attaching any wires (and she double checked that) she began to play with the buttons in a variety of combinations. She managed to get the display to light up, then to get numbers to appear on it. Petra guessed that was the countdown. The numbers appeared in two two-digit displays, like a minutes and seconds counter. A completely different switch sat on the side of the detonator. She guessed that would start the countdown. What she knew for sure was that no one would design a detonator that would instantly blow up a charge that was sitting a few feet from your face.

With the detonator figured out, she had maneuvered the boat to the narrowest point of the atoll ring. With a blast of full power, she'd run the boat ashore where the ridge between the waters was lowest. The last steps would be to inflate the raft, set the timer, abandon ship, and run before the big boom.

She convinced herself that she had a handle on this. Now, as the boat bobbed off shore, it was time to put the plan in motion.

Petra took the charge and laid it against the bulkhead in the bow. She attached the two wires from the detonator to the charge and double-checked that they were tight. She took a deep breath, and pushed the green button.

The four red timer digits blinked to life. Nothing exploded. So far so good.

She pushed the two buttons on the top and the numbers in the first two positions started to increment up. When it got to five, she released the buttons. Five minutes would be plenty of time to get out of the boat and run outside the blast radius. She wondered if Marie had made it to the beach yet.

Petra set down the detonator and went to the pilothouse. She climbed up and stuck her head through the open hatch. A scan across the beach revealed a woman standing on the ridge to her left. She didn't know what Marie looked like, but that had to be her. It wasn't like this atoll was crawling with busloads of tourists.

Petra aimed the boat for the shore and then pushed the throttle to wide open. The engine ramped up to a low whine and the bow rose. The boat sped forward and closed rapidly on the beach. Just ahead, a large roller was beginning to crest on its way ashore. Petra aimed the boat for its peak. The boat caught the wave and rode it into the beach. The hull landed on the sand keel first. The sudden stop tried to throw Petra into the cupola, but she'd braced herself against it. The boat settled a few degrees to starboard. Petra had beached the semi-submersible right where she'd aimed it.

Out to the left, Marie started to head down the ridge. Petra popped open the hatch and climbed out. She shouted a warning and waved Marie off with both hands. No point in both of them sprinting back up the ridge she was already on top of. Marie paused.

Petra went to the stern and uncased the life raft. Her damaged, throbbing shoulder reminded her that she was way overdue for proper medical care. With its bow line under one foot, she pulled the inflation handle and rolled it off the side. The yellow block expanded into a life raft. A light began to flash from a box in the stern, indicating that the distress signal had started to transmit to Green Warriors' mothership. Their ride home would soon be here.

Petra flashed Marie another hand signal to wait on the ridge, and then she jumped down and dragged the raft well out of what would be the blast zone. She ran back to the boat, climbed down inside, and went back to the bow. She patted the explosive charge with a smile on her face.

"Now you get to make a nice big boom."

She threw the switch on the side. The two numbers on the right side of the display counted down so fast she could barely read them. The five on the display changed to a four. In an instant, that four changed to a three.

"Oh crap." She realized the numbers didn't count down minutes, they counted down seconds. She froze in panic as the three on the display changed to a two.

She pushed the switch on the side to turn off the counter. It broke off in her fingers. The two on the display changed to a one.

She reached down and grabbed the wires to yank them out of the charge. She pulled hard. The wires didn't break. Instead, they pulled the charge away from the bulkhead. It landed at her feet.

The display number changed to zero.

Marie had figured out that the plan must have changed. Maybe the sub was damaged, so they were going to get off the island on the raft Petra had just inflated. But she should have been back out of the boat by now.

Marie was about to start down the ridge again when the boat erupted in a massive explosion. Burning boards and shredded fiberglass arced across the sky. A fireball erupted from the bow and spread thirty yards in all directions. A split-second later a thunderclap boom vibrated her joints and made her cover her ears. Then a concussion wave so strong that it was visible rolled out across sand and sea. It roared up the ridge and knocked Marie down with a wall of gritty sand particles.

She wiped the ashy sand from her face and checked the beach. The burning stern of the boat stuck out of the water, but the rest of the boat was just a blackened outline flecked with flames. Where the bow had been, a huge crater now gouged the beach. Waves sent seawater waterfalling into its depths.

Then the wall of the crater closest to the lagoon collapsed and created a gap in the ridge about three feet wide. Water from the lagoon began to rush through it, feeding the crater and mixing with the incoming tide. The outgoing lagoon water scoured sand from the sides of the ridge. Every incoming wave drew that sand out to sea. The break would only get wider and deeper from here.

Marie smiled. Petra had somehow screwed up and turned herself into a giant pipe bomb, but she'd accomplished something amazing. She'd blown open the atoll, allowing the monsters within to enter the sea. She'd be sure Green Warriors gave Petra a medal or whatever they did to commemorate those who died for their cause. For right now, Marie's job was to stay off that list of martyrs.

She glanced behind her at the open lagoon. Rothman was dead in his sunken seabase. His dreams for Atoll X had died with him. Nirvana Island would be abandoned. And once the monsters in this lagoon were out ravaging the ocean's commercial fisheries, Rothman's legacy would be forever destroyed.

She laughed thinking that at one point she would have settled for just poisoning him.

Her big yellow ticket off this awful atoll sat on the beach below her. She even had two options. Petra said that the mothership was waiting somewhere nearby to evacuate Petra and her now-dead team. Marie would use her satellite phone to call Green Warriors and have them send the ship in to pick her up instead. In no time, she would be back home.

If she couldn't raise Green Warriors, she could just paddle back to Nirvana Island. By the time she got there, she'd have a splendid story concocted about how she heroically tried to save all the people who perished in Rothman's seabase folly.

All the sanctimonious preachers had been wrong. She could now testify from experience that revenge was exceptionally satisfying.

CHAPTER THIRTY-FOUR

Grant stood stunned at what he'd just seen. The pseudo-submarine had beached itself and blown up, generating a fireball worthy of a Hollywood blockbuster. Black smoke now rose from the half-submerged stern of the boat. A small, but widening, gap that joined the lagoon and the sea was the opening act of an awful tragedy.

"Waves and lagoon water are going to turn that sluice into a channel pretty quickly," Irina said.

"This will be an ecological catastrophe like the world has never seen," Grant said. "Ichthyosaurs running unchecked in the open ocean will instantly become the South Pacific's apex predator."

"And they dive deeper and stay underwater longer than even whales." Irina wobbled and then steadied herself. "They'll multiply faster than mankind could ever hunt them, if we could find them at all."

"The good news is," Grant said, "we'll be eaten by giant crocodiles long before we have to see all those repercussions come to pass."

Marie was making her way down the ridge on the other side of the tear in the lagoon wall. She was making a beeline for the yellow raft the person in the submarine had deployed. To top off her sinking of the seabase, it looked like she had a hand in this ensuing environmental catastrophe as well.

"We have to plug that gap." Irina pointed to the skiff on the lagoon's shore. "I'll go down and—"

Irina's eyes rolled up in her head. Her knees buckled. Grant caught her and eased her to the ground. He laid her down and scooped a pillow of sand to support her head.

Her eyes fluttered back open. "Hey! I know you."

"Don't move," Grant said. "Your concussion is bad."

She nodded and closed her eyes again.

Grant knew they did have to plug the break in the atoll. But how? She'd pointed to the skiff. Grant looked at the widening gap in the lagoon shore. The water surged back and forth through it faster. He looked back at the skiff. It was larger than the gap. If it got there quickly, it would work like a cork. Even if it just slowed the flow enough to stop the gap from widening, nothing bigger than a minnow was going to get out of the lagoon. Someone just had to get the skiff into that gap.

And that someone was going to have to be him.

"When is Fate going to figure out that I'm not the heroic type?" he muttered.

He made a skidding, barely controlled descent down the berm to the skiff at the base. He pushed it out into the water and with a clumsy half-roll managed to get himself over the side and into the boat. Winded and wet, he really wished all of this was over. He crawled to behind the steering wheel and a press of a button brought the engine to life. He aimed the boat into the lagoon, so that he could drive it bow-first into the gap to the ocean.

Something big splashed out in the lagoon and he remembered how much ichthyosaurs seemed to hate him.

Grant sent the boat into a tight turn and rolled out heading for the gap, a hundred yards away. He pushed the throttle wide open and the engine roared.

Halfway between him and the shore, a giant ichthyosaur breached the surface. It was twice the size of the one that had attacked the station and the tube he'd escaped in. Its head rose six feet out of the water and its malignant obsidian eye stared down Grant in his little boat. The reptile crashed back down into the water. It disappeared but the impact sent two large waves rolling out in opposite directions. One of them headed straight for Grant.

He gritted his teeth, gripped the steering wheel, and wished for the umpteenth time during this trip that he was a better swimmer. The wave rolled under the boat and sent the bow so high that suddenly all Grant could see was sky. As the wave passed, the boat fell like it had been dropped from a plane. The bow crashed into the water. White spray drenched the cockpit and fogged his glasses. Grant's jaw slammed shut and he bit his tongue. The sharp sound of cracking fiberglass accompanied a shudder that wracked the whole hull. The stern popped out of the water and the engine screamed as the propellers cut through nothing but air.

The stern dropped down and the engine's shaft dug back into the water. The prop growled as it tried to get the boat back up to speed. Grant wiped the worst of the water from his glasses and re-aimed the boat at the gap.

Another splash sounded from behind him. He turned to see a huge ichthyosaur dorsal fin cutting through the lagoon, heading for his boat.

Grant's heart began to gallop. He leaned on the throttle, as if he could push the boat forward a bit faster by doing so. He was a dozen yards from the gap, but the ichthyosaur was closing fast.

A glance over the side revealed shallowing water as Grant approached the lagoon's edge. The creature was huge. Hope that the ichthyosaur couldn't follow him this close to shore caught fire. He might live through this.

He looked back up. In his panic, he'd forgotten to slow the boat's approach. Sand was just feet away, and the boat still screamed at top speed. His pounding heart stopped.

The boat slammed into the gap in the berm. The impact threw Grant over the steering wheel and past the bow. He landed with a splash in the hole the exploded boat had made. He looked back. Through his water-dappled lenses, he saw the ichthyosaur leaping out of the lagoon, aimed for the boat. Grant's body locked up in terror.

The ichthyosaur crashed down on the skiff. It exploded into a thousand bits of shattered fiberglass. The engine coughed and died as the reptile's belly pressed it into the sand. The tip of its jaws was inches from Grant's face. The creature stank like an untended fish tank. It snapped at Grant and missed.

Grant scrambled away and up the berm. He wiped his glasses and got a better view of the ichthyosaur. The creature lay in the berm gap, out of the water save the ends of its tail. Its body heaved as it tried to breathe. Ichthyosaurs were air breathers, but while surrounded by water. Exposed on land, it seemed to be unable to keep its lungs expanded. Flippers beat uselessly at the sand as it tried to pull itself forward to the ocean that offered it relief.

The creature stopped moving. Its black eye rolled around to stare one last time at Grant, then it went glassy and dimmed.

The boat probably would have been a terrible plug for the gap between the lagoon and the sea. The ichthyosaur carcass was a perfect one. The water flow between the two bodies stopped.

Grant made his way back to Irina. He was certain that now his bruises had bruises. When he stood over her, she opened her eyes.

"You made it." Irina sounded stronger.

"Yes, still not dead. Can't say that for the ichthyosaur plugging the gap in the berm, though."

Then the ground beneath his feet rumbled. From the lagoon came the sound of a huge, muffled explosion.

Out in the water, circular ripples expanded from the lagoon's center.

A great, white circle of foam formed in the middle of the lagoon. It swelled like an enormous mushroom fifty yards across. It rose almost as high, pushing a dead ichthyosaur atop its crown. Then it dropped back into the lagoon.

"That was the engineering section imploding?" Grant said.

"No," Irina said. "That was the reactor core exploding, or at least releasing enough instantaneous energy to superheat the lagoon water around it."

Steam began to rise from the lagoon. Ichthyosaurs breached the surface like sailfish on a fisherman's line, a dozen of all different sizes. They crashed back into the simmering water and high-pitched shrieks echoed between the shores.

"They're cooking alive," Grant said. "Reptiles are not good at regulating their body heat, especially when they are adapted to a near uniform environment like the sea."

"I'm going to guess that dumping all that concentrated salt waste isn't doing them any favors either."

Schools of smaller dead fish popped to the lagoon surface like blooming lilies.

"Welcome to the world's biggest seafood boil," Grant said. "I'm not eating any of the radioactive results, though."

"The contamination will be minimal," Irina said. "The reactor is small and the worst of it is well underwater. I doubt you've even been dosed with the equivalent of an X-ray."

"I'm still not signing up for the timeshare option here."

Then Grant thought he saw something out to the south in the ocean. At first, he dismissed it as a cresting wave in the sea, but when it didn't go away, he knew it had to be something else.

"Is that a boat?" he asked, pointing out to sea.

Irina sat up and shaded her eyes from the sun. A smile spread across her face. 'Hell, yeah, that's a boat!"

"All it took was a burning boat and a nuclear detonation to get someone's attention. Why didn't we just do that in the first place?"

"Well, they won't find us up here. Let's get to the beach."

Grant reached down to help Irina up. "I'm ready to swim out to the boat, and I hate swimming."

What he didn't see on the water was the yellow raft Marie had used to get off the atoll. It looked like she'd gotten away scot-free.

CHAPTER THIRTY-FIVE

The warm sun and salt air kissed Marie's face as she rowed across the waves, skirting the atoll's northeastern shore. There were so few moments in life where great dreams were realized that she decided to relish this one as long as possible.

She took out her satellite phone and turned it on to call the mothership about the rendezvous. It didn't turn on. She flicked the switch a few times, then smacked it against the boat. Nothing.

Maybe it had gotten wet. Maybe the blast impact from the pseudo-sub had fried it. Maybe the battery was just dead. It would have been nice to let the mothership know exactly where she was, but it would all work itself out anyway. The blinking light on the emergency transponder box in the bow would be sending out the deep-sea equivalent of calling for an Uber.

A few large boulders poked from the sea ahead, so she steered the skiff a bit further away from the atoll. She remembered the giant crocodiles and figured that was another good reason to stay away from the shore. She certainly didn't need to have this wonderful day end by being eaten by a giant monster.

She rounded the eastern shore of the atoll and headed west. Up ahead, a little further out to sea, she spotted a boat. The transponder call had worked! She wouldn't even be spending the day out on the water.

She closed on the boat and recognized it as an oceangoing fishing trawler. She'd seen environmentalist groups use ships like that disrupting oil drilling and whale hunts. According to the crab catching shows she'd watched, the accommodations weren't first class, but she'd be fine with any transportation back to civilization.

Further down the coast, a second boat appeared. Marie's smile crumbled. She recognized that boat as well. It was the pirate craft that had driven the *Endeavor* ashore in the first place. She'd already seen this movie, and wasn't in a hurry for a second viewing.

She dug in her heels and rowed harder for the trawler. The pirate craft was faster, but she was closer to the trawler than it was. She thought she could make it. Once there, she'd be safe. A bunch of eco-warriors who could send in a submarine of armed arsonists would be able to fend off a boat of pirates.

The raft struggled through the swells toward the trawler. She made out the silhouettes of two people on the bow, who pointed at her boat and shouted something to the pilothouse.

That's it, she thought. *Roll out the red carpet.*

The pirate ship closed faster than she expected. The idea that she might not make it crossed her mind. She pointed the oars deeper into the water and put her back into the effort.

Aboard the pirate ship, a man ran up to the bow carrying an assault rifle. He took aim at Marie's raft and fired. The bullet fell far short of her boat, but the message made it all the way to her. They were coming for her.

She got close enough to make out more details on the trawler. No national flag flew from the ship, just as she'd expected. The name on the bow had been painted over with flat black paint. Like a gift from above, a rope ladder hung from the side near the stern. She could scramble to safety in seconds. If she had seconds to spare.

She checked the distance to the pirate boat. She wasn't going to make it. Even if the boat didn't get to her before she reached the trawler, bullets from the pirate's rifle surely would. She scream in frustration. Her story couldn't possibly end this way.

She was only a dozen feet from the trawler when the pirate veered left and peeled away in a wide arc. Marie shouted triumph.

"Don't want to tangle with any true bad-asses, do you?" s shouted at the pirates. "Anything more than a woman in an open raft scares the hell out of you."

She pulled in the oars as she approached the trawler. The raft bumped against the hull and she grabbed the rope ladder. Marie pulled herself out of the raft. A glance over her shoulder revealed that the pirate boat had come to a stop about eighty yards from the trawler. The men on it were lined up along the side, watching her.

She wished she could spit in their faces. This made twice she'd gotten away from them.

She started to climb and as she looked up, a face appeared over the railing. Marie froze on the ladder.

Above her, a man with skin tanned to leather stared down at her. He wore a baseball cap backwards and had a nasty, thick scar running down his left cheek. He smiled and revealed two gold teeth. He was the same man who'd captained the pirate skiff earlier. She hadn't boarded a safe haven; she'd climbed into Hell.

From across the water, the pirates in the smaller boat started laughing.

CHAPTER THIRTY-SIX

Later that evening, Grant sat alone on the patio beside the empty pool at the unfinished Nirvana Island resort. He'd bet his next year's pay that after the last few days, the resort would remain that way.

The sun had about an hour before it would dip below the palms behind the resort and clock out for the day. Grant planned on following the sun's example. He felt like he hadn't slept in days, and for good reason. He hadn't. He'd also burned through a year's supply of adrenaline at the same time. He planned on sleeping through all of tomorrow.

Just to make sure he did, he had enlisted some help. A longneck beer bottle stuck out of a bucket of melting ice beside him. He'd brought it and a now empty brother out here after dinner. Without Marie in the kitchen, the food was marginal. Grant's suffering palette was another reason her betrayal stung hard.

Irina stepped through the doors and out to the patio. She had a tall mixed drink in one hand. She went over to Grant, collapsed into the chair beside him, and put her drink beside his beer bucket.

"Should you be drinking with a concussion?" Grant said.

"I'll soon find out," Irina said.

"There's no skewered fruit in that drink," Grant said. "You're approaching this drinking as serious business."

"After the last two days, I may never stop drinking."

"How did the conference call go in there?"

"It took an hour to convince the Board of Directors that I worked for Rothman," she said. "Then I couldn't finish two sentences without someone stopping me to say what I'd just told them was impossible. Would I make all that up? Say, I bet you never thought you'd be living through encounters with giant monsters."

"Oddly, I've come to expect it."

Irina gave him a quizzical look.

"Just kidding," Grant said.

"A whole collection of top officers in the organization and a dozen lawyers are flying to Tonga now. Carla will fly them out to Nirvana Island and then she'll take you back to Tonga. You have a flight back to the States in the afternoon."

"I can't say I'll be sorry to go."

"They indicated you are going to be well-compensated for signing a draconian non-disclosure agreement."

"I'll hold out for double whatever they offer."

"They'll pay it," Irina said. "Do you think any ichthyosaurs survived in the lagoon?"

"I doubt anything survived. We turned it into a pretty toxic brew. With that part of the ecosystem destroyed, I wouldn't lay odds on the salamanders or crocodiles surviving for long either."

"Just in case, the company is sending in hunters to clean up any surviving megafauna. From helicopters, of course."

"If they want an Atoll X tour guide," Grant said, "don't knock on my door. Relatives of all the people who died have been notified?"

"All except Marie. She wasn't who she said she was. Her fiancé was killed by an autonomous vehicle from a Rothman corporation. No one caught that in her background check. They think she may have had a grudge against Rothman."

"Think so? Someone put some serious detective work into that conclusion."

"Do you think she got away?"

"Who knows," Grant said. "It will catch up to her eventually. Things like this always do."

"Your plans?" Irina said.

"Go back to my teaching job and never leave the campus again."

Irina patted his hand. "You did pretty good out there for a college professor. You pulled your own weight."

"Is that a fat joke?"

"God, no. A real-life compliment."

"They are so few and far between," Grant said, "that I rarely recognize them. Is anyone contemplating finishing Rothman's vanity project here?"

"Not really. All the bigwigs want to see everything for themselves, but the economics of this place were dicey from the start, and no one seemed to have the stomach for finishing it, especially given what went on at Atoll X."

"And what are their plans for you?" Grant said.

"I guess I'll find out tomorrow. But whatever they finally agree to as payment for your NDA, I'm asking for double that."

"Ask for triple. Go big or go home."

Irina raised her glass to Grant. "Here's to going big *and* going home."

Grant clinked his bottle against her glass. "I'll drink to that."

CHAPTER THIRTY-SEVEN

Six months later

Grant set the stack of test papers aside on his desk, removed his glasses and rubbed his eyes. Fighting off killer ichthyosaurs was a miserable, heart-pounding experience, but the monotonous drudgery of test grading had its own set of drawbacks. He certainly preferred the happy place in between where he was at a dig, calmly unearthing fossils from the ground.

The desk phone rang. The caller ID revealed the caller was his agent, Harvey Rindzunner. Grant picked up the phone.

"Harvey!" Grant said. "What a surprise."

"I told you I'd call today," Harvey said.

"That's what makes it such a surprise. You usually lie about that."

"Grant, you wound me with your words. Deeply. Especially when I am bringing you such good news. I sold *Atoll X* to the publisher and got you a sweet advance."

That was good news. Grant had written the thinly-veiled autobiographical story of his Pacific atoll adventure after he'd returned. As fiction, it skirted the edge of his NDA. Despite the fact that most of the events were true, he was afraid they would be too unbelievable to get published, even in a novel.

"The editors asked me," Harvey said, "these giant monsters you keep coming up with, where do you get the inspiration?"

"You know, I'm just minding my own business, leading a normal life, and then suddenly they appear right in front of me."

"Well, do whatever you need to do to keep those inspirational moments coming."

Grant would really rather that he didn't. A monster-free future would suit him just fine.

"I got a line on a consulting gig for your semester break," Harvey said. "There's a guy in—"

"Stop right there," Grant cut him off. "The mess in the Pacific ended your vacation planner status for me. You just keep scaring up publishing and media deals. If I want to go somewhere, I'll search through an online booking agency."

"This is easy money."

"That's what you said about Nirvana Island. Hard pass."

"You're killing me, Grant." A phone rang in the background. "Gotta get that call. Talk later."

Harvey hung up.

Grant's boss, Dean Malley, entered Grant's office. The stooped, older man had a long nose that Grant thought spent too much time being poked into his curriculum and teaching methods. He wore a dark suit sporting a plastic breast pocket name badge adorned with the college logo. The dean only wore that badge when he was greeting alumni, which reminded Grant that there had been an alumni luncheon that day, which reminded Grant he was supposed to have attended it.

"Dean Malley! Your unannounced visits are always a treat."

"You missed the alumni luncheon. I'm disappointed in you."

"As am I. It's not like me to forget about free food."

"Making alumni contacts will go a long way in helping keep your employer well-funded, you know."

"I've seen the size of Robeson University's endowment," Grant said. "Contrary to what the size of my paycheck would indicate, the university isn't broke."

"One of the alumni announced he was sponsoring a geological study in the Southwest," Dean Malley said. "He appointed Casey Palmer to lead it."

Professor Casey Palmer and Grant were friends. Casey was the university's top geology professor and frequently did consulting work.

"Maybe if you networked with the alumni more," Dean Malley said, "someone might steer an opportunity like that your way."

Grant wanted to reply that the last "opportunity" he'd just experienced had damn near killed him on several occasions. "I'll keep that in mind."

"Another high-profile expedition would sure make me proud."

"Making you proud is my whole reason for living," Grant said.

Dean Malley rolled his eyes and left. A few minutes later, Casey Palmer entered Grant's office. He was Grant's age but taller, leaner, and with a touch of gray to his hair. He was beaming.

"You weren't at the luncheon," he said.

"You're the second person to be concerned about me missing a meal. Do I look emaciated?"

"Hardly. But I did get some good news there."

"That you'll be leading an all-expense paid trip to study rocks in the desert?"

Casey's eyes widened. "How did you know? It was just announced."

"Crystal ball. Tea leaves. Chicken bones. I have my ways."

"You can't know the best part of the deal. You get to come along, all expenses paid as well."

"And why would I want to go look at rocks in the desert?" Grant said.

"Along with the geology they told me about, the company has found where some earthquakes exposed some interesting fossils in this remote desert canyon."

Grant's ears perked up and he set down his pen. Having had enough of oceans, lagoons, and murderous aquatic life to last a lifetime, the desert sounded wonderful. And he'd just been thinking how much he missed the thrill of fossil discovery. "That offer sounds interesting."

"The expedition is going to a spot called Desolation Canyon, in an area northeast of the Grand Canyon complex. The sponsor doesn't care about fossils, and I'm betting they'll let you take any you find back to the university."

Now Grant was very interested. Some new fossils would keep him and his grad students engaged and excited for over a semester.

"Look," Casey said, "I'll email you all the details and make all the travel arrangements. It will be great!"

Casey departed. Grant turned to his computer and called up a map of Nevada. He couldn't find anywhere named Desolation Canyon. In fact, a lot of the area northeast of the Grand Canyon was just a big empty space on the map, without even any real terrain details to it. Whatever was there, no one had likely seen it before.

After his Atoll X nightmare, this trip would be the perfect tonic. Dry, quiet, and above all, monster-free. What could go wrong?

He realized that was the same thought he had before he left to go to Nirvana Island.

AFTERWORD

Well, that wasn't the relaxing trip to the South Pacific Grant hoped for, was it? I have a feeling this poor guy could be attacked by giant monsters visiting his local duck pond.

I try to use a lot of facts to create credible science fiction. Without a little grounding in reality, I'd be writing fantasy. My goal is to give you a story that's just credible enough that you only have to suspend a sliver of disbelief. So, let's go over some of the facts that support this round of fiction.

First off, I'll confess that Atoll X might not technically be an atoll at all.

An atoll is a ring-shaped coral reef, island, or series of islets that surround a lagoon. They are found in the Pacific and Indian oceans. Atoll formation begins when a volcano erupts on the ocean floor and expels enough lava to rise above the sea and create an island. Corals then build what's called a fringing reef around the island.

Over millions of years, the volcanic island erodes and leaves only a barrier reef and the lagoon within. Eventually, ocean waves grind the coral into tiny grains of sand that accumulate on the reef, forming a ring-shaped island or islets.

I couldn't very well set a story on a true atoll. They are usually quite small, barren, and could never support the fun creatures I wanted to have Grant engage. Atoll X is an earlier version of an atoll. The volcano has created an island in the Pacific, but then a catastrophic eruption like at Mt. St. Helen has blasted away the top and left a deep crater that filled with seawater to create a lagoon. Rising and falling sea levels left ichthyosaurs isolated like fish in a tide pool, and *voila*, giant monster story. The dead volcano scenario allowed me to have an island that could support larger creatures, much to Grant's chagrin.

The lagoon's apex predator is the ichthyosaur. The first ichthyosaurs appeared in the Triassic, peaked in evolution and numbers in the Jurassic, and then disappeared in the Cretaceous.

The ichthyosaurs in the story are modeled after actual species, which did resemble large dolphins in a process called parallel evolution, where a naturally advantageous design becomes dominant in different species.

Ichthyosaurs bore live young, breathed air, and one fossil find in 2018 is believed to have traces of blubber under the well-preserved skin. The largest fossil ever found measured in at 85 feet long. As a quick reference, that's four times the size of a killer whale.

My fictional ichthyosaurs stay underwater for a long time, but not unrealistically long compared to living reptiles. Sea turtles hold the record, and can stay underwater for days when resting. On average, even active sea turtles can hold their breath for up to seven hours.

Grant and company also meet up with giant saltwater crocodiles. One of the largest ever to bask in the sand was *Deinosuchus* (Latin for "terror crocodile" like that isn't redundant) and he clocked in at 33 feet, or almost as long as a school bus. They had teeth the size of bananas and jaws with the strength to crush good-sized dinosaurs. Modern saltwater crocodiles have the strongest recorded bite of any living animal, fifty times stronger than a human being. *Deinosuchus* could have been four times stronger than a modern croc. These things could likely out-crush a *Tyrannosaurus*.

Australia hosts the largest, deadliest type of living saltwater croc, more proof of my theory that every wild animal in Australia wants to kill me. They grow to 20 feet long and can swim at 20 miles per hour. Humans win Olympic gold medals at 4.7 miles per hour by comparison. Swim at your own risk.

Lastly, we have our cute-but-nasty venomous salamanders. Venomous reptiles are relatively common, from poisonous snakes (some of which can spit without biting) to tree frogs that sweat poison onto their skin to deter being eaten. Could a salamander really have a tongue that long? Well, the amphibian with the longest tongue is a Sardinian cave dwelling salamander named *Hydromantes supramontis*. They are typically about five inches long, and their tongues are over four inches long, or 80% of their body length. Researching all these creatures may someday keep me from ever venturing outdoors.

Kaelo fashions the group Tongan war clubs to defend themselves. Such weapons have been part of Tongan society since long before Western contact. Though they evolved to much more ceremonial uses, initially they were serious combat weapons. In real life it is a much more elaborate process to create one and they are best made from hardwoods that would be tough to hand carve with a knife.

Rothman's seabase was inspired by my favorite long-gone ride at Disney's EPCOT theme park. The Living Seas was a very realistic simulation that put you into the "hydrolator" and delivered you to an underwater science research station called Seabase Alpha, where you could look out on an enormous aquarium with sharks, dolphins, sea turtles and a host of other species swimming around. There were also a lot of other fish on display in smaller settings. Now it's been mutated into a Finding Nemo ride, though the aquarium is still there.

The Green Warriors' semi-submersible is modeled after actual boats like that used by drug kingpins for smuggling.

Thanks go out to my wonderful beta readers Deb DeAlteriis and Donna Fitzpatrick for taste testing this latest adventure and recommending some wonderful changes to the seasoning. Thanks also to the great folks at Severed Press for turning the kaiju niche into a viable business and giving Grant the chance to bumble his way through his adventures.

I would never have embarked on this particular writing journey unless I was certain that I could keep Kaelo's character and background true-to-life. I am forever in debt to Daphne Maxson Wolfgramm and Koloti Lamisitoni Wolfgramm, two champions of Tongan culture for starting me off with amazing background information and for double-checking my use of it.

Special thanks go out to all of you out there reading my books. You are responsible for me being able to do what I love for a living. Watch my website and social media for the next convention I am attending and please come by and say hello. It is always a pleasure to meet all of you.

Seems that Grant has survived another brush with giant monsters. Will his trip to uncharted Desolation Canyon be danger-free? We'll see what happens, but given his luck, I doubt it. In the meantime, you can entertain yourself with the adventures of Rangers Kathy West and Nathan Toland who fight to keep dangerous creatures at bay in the United States National Park system. In *Claws* they battle giant crabs at Fort Jefferson in the Florida Keys. In *Dragons of Kilauea,* fire-breathing giant Komodo dragons threaten Volcanoes National Park in Hawaii. In their latest adventure, *Ravens of Yellowstone,* they discover the secrets of the park system's formation while uncovering a roost of murderous birds about to be set free. All are available from Severed Press at booksellers around the world.

Stay well and keep reading. I'll go check on what kind of trouble Grant has gotten himself into.

-Russell James

CHECK OUT OTHER GREAT DEEP SEA THRILLERS

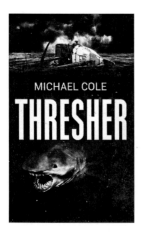

THRESHER
by Michael Cole

In the aftermath of a hurricane, a series of strange events plague the coastal waters off Florida. People go into the water and never return. Corpses of killer whales drift ashore, ravaged from enormous bite marks. A fishing trawler is found adrift, with a mysterious gash in its hull.

Transferred to the coastal town of Merit, police officer Leonard Riker uncovers the horrible reality of an enormous Thresher shark lurking off the coast. Forty feet in length, it has taken a territorial claim to the waters near the town harbor. Armed with three-inch teeth, a scythe-like caudal fin, and unmatched aggression, the beast seeks to kill anything sharing the waters.

THE GUILLOTINE
by Lucas Pederson

1,000 feet under the surface, Prehistoric Anthropologist, Ash Barrington, and his team are in the midst of a great archeological dig at the bottom of Lake Superior where they find a treasure trove of bones. Bones of dinosaurs that aren't supposed to be in this particular region. In their underwater facility, Infinity Moon, Ash and his team soon discover a series of underground tunnels. Upon exploring, they accidentally open an ice pocket, thawing the prehistoric creature trapped inside. Soon they are being attacked, the facility falling apart around them, by what Ash knows is a dunkleosteus and all those bones were from its prey. Now...Ash and his team are the prey and the creature will stop at nothing to get to them.

CHECK OUT OTHER GREAT DEEP SEA THRILLERS

THE BREACH
by Edward J. McFadden III

A Category 4 hurricane punched a quarter mile hole in Fire Island, exposing the Great South Bay to the ferocity of the Atlantic Ocean, and the current pulled something terrible through the new breach. A monstrosity of the past mixed with the present has been disturbed and it's found its way into the sheltered waters of Long Island's southern sea.

Nate Tanner lives in Stones Throw, Long Island. A disgraced SCPD detective lieutenant put out to pasture in the marine division because of his Navy background and experience with aquatic crime scenes, Tanner is assigned to hunt the creeper in the bay. But he and his team soon discover they're the ones being hunted.

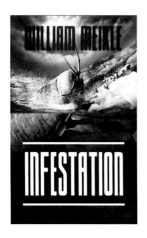

INFESTATION
by William Meikle

It was supposed to be a simple mission. A suspected Russian spy boat is in trouble in Canadian waters. Investigate and report are the orders.

But when Captain John Banks and his squad arrive, it is to find an empty vessel, and a scene of bloody mayhem.

Soon they are in a fight for their lives, for there are things in the icy seas off Baffin Island, scuttling, hungry things with a taste for human flesh.

They are swarming. And they are growing.

"Scotland's best Horror writer" - Ginger Nuts of Horror

"The premier storyteller of our time." - Famous Monsters of Filmland

Check out other great
Sea Monster Novels!

Rick Chesler
HOTEL MEGALODON

An underwater luxury hotel on a gorgeous tropical island is set for an extravagant opening weekend with the world watching. The only thing standing in the way of a first-rate experience for the jet-setting VIPs is an unscrupulous businessman and sixty feet of prehistoric shark. As the underwater complex is besieged by a marauding behemoth, newly minted marine biologist Coco Keahi must face off against the ancient predator as it rises from the deep with a vengeance. Meanwhile, a human monster has decided he would be better off if Coco were one of the creature's victims.

Michael Cole
SCAR

Scar is a killing machine. Born from DNA spliced between the extinct Megalodon and modern day Great White, he has a viciousness that transcends time. His evil is reflected in his eyes, his savagery in his two-inch serrated teeth, his ruthlessness in his trail of death. After escaping captivity, the killer shark travels to the island community Cross Point, where prey is in abundance. With an insatiable appetite, heightened senses, and skin impervious to bullets, Scar kills everything that crosses his path. His reign of terror puts him at war with the island sheriff, Nick Piatt. With the body count rising, Nick vows to protect his island community from the vicious threat. With the aid of a marine biologist, a rookie deputy, and a bad-tempered fisherman, Nick leads a crusade against Scar, as well as the ruthless scientist who created him.

Made in United States
North Haven, CT
31 March 2024